Magic:
The Power of Tel-ana

Harold Ray

Order this book online at www.trafford.com
or email orders@trafford.com

Most Trafford titles are also available at major online book retailers.

Printed in Victoria, BC, Canada.

ISBN: 978-1-4269-1429-4 (Soft)

*We at Trafford believe that it is the responsibility of us all, as both individuals
and corporations, to make choices that are environmentally and socially sound.
You, in turn, are supporting this responsible conduct each time you purchase a
Trafford book, or make use of our publishing services. To find out how you are
helping, please visit www.trafford.com/responsiblepublishing.html*

*Our mission is to efficiently provide the world's finest, most comprehensive
book publishing service, enabling every author to experience success.
To find out how to publish your book, your way, and have it available
worldwide, visit us online at www.trafford.com*

Trafford rev. 12/17/2009

 www.trafford.com

North America & international
toll-free: 1 888 232 4444 (USA & Canada)
phone: 250 383 6864 ♦ fax: 812 355 4082 ♦ email: info@trafford.com

In the Time of Beginning, the Guardians oversaw chaos, savages reigned and heretics defiled their good name. The Guardians descended and bestowed upon the True Believers their eternal gifts that they and their descendants shall receive forever.

In the Time of Beginning, the Guardians waged war with the savages. The savages cowered before the might of the Guardians. Those who did not repent to the Guardians were driven into darkness.

In the Time of Beginning, the Guardians saw what they did and it was good. They then ascended beyond where they shall remain beyond the edge of time.

There exists the most powerful Guardian weapon in the world of Tel-ana. None can recall the title. Modern Sages have titled it 'Geddon.' Neither magic nor physical attacks can hurt it. Only the Guardian Journal in Morbia can summon it.

Translation
-Journal of the Guardian Iber
Under the protectorate of
Sage Mattonda Giersi, Iberia

I dedicate this book to my family, whose intelligence, personality, and experience have not only influenced my writing, but influenced me personally.

The world of Tel-ána is a world where magic is as real as the humans that inhabit it. This magic was a gift from the Guardians, the gods who oversaw everything. The Guardians gave them magic, which according to legend originated from the Guardians' own power, for defeating enemies that have long since been forgotten from written history. The Guardians determine each human's magic attribute at birth based on the individual's soul and destiny. Three months after the person is born, their magic is then assessed by masters called Sages who determine the potential of each magic attribute. There is very little, if any, cost or drawback to this magic and people are free to use it as they wish. However, sometimes people use it to harm others, as is the case with all societies with power. So the Sages also serve as protectors, guarding the people from harmful magic and guarding those who would want to defy the Guardians' will by illegally acquiring other magic. The Sages were so powerful that they even serve as advisors to the rulers of Tel-ána and were rarely betrayed.

The world of Tel-ána is divided into kingdoms, each connected by a gateway. These gateways stand five times the size of a human and can only be parted by a wheelie and control system and guarded by soldiers from both of the kingdoms that share the gate. There are a total of eleven known kingdoms in Tel-ána: Sanchair, Kashuto, Morbia, Iberia, Costal Glen, Mishanko, Estrellia, Vernaclia, Boscov, Jargon, and Pasornin. There is also a dark region that is considered unknown territory because nobody in current times has visited it. However, it is considered a kingdom nonetheless. Most of Tel-ána has named this place Darinka, an ancient word meaning dark land due to the fact that the clouds overshadowing it have shrouded it in an eternal night. The kingdoms themselves consist of a castle within the capitol city along with various small towns and villages, each surrounded by a large wooden fence. The castles are of various shapes, sizes, and features. For example, the Sanchair Kingdom is surrounded by a large chasm with a bridge of light connecting it to the rest of the land. That bridge disappears every day at sunset and appears again at sunrise.

Everybody is part of a kingdom with the possible exception of Darinka. For a while, tensions were running high between the kingdoms and fifteen years before the time that our story takes place in, a war broke out between two rivaling kingdoms. After a bloody conflict, the tension between them as well as the other kingdoms dissolved to a low boil. There are still some hostilities between some kingdoms but nothing to cause a big ruckus like what happened fifteen years prior, at least for now. However, as in all societies, there are some people who live for death and destruction. Tel-ána was no exception. But just as there would be people who abuse magic, so would there be people who protect magic and people who are merely caught in the wrong place at the wrong time. It is with one of those latter people that our story begins.

Marta is a young girl living in the isolated village of Gerard in the Iberian Kingdom. Although she had only recently turned twelve, Marta was rapidly developing her magical abilities. At her birth, a Sage concluded that her magic was a rare one, a magic only held by a select few people. Using a series of movements with her hands, and feet, almost like a dance, Marta could vibrate the air around her causing a shockwave with various degrees of severity. At her current age, her so-called "vibro-shocks" could knock someone down and almost render that person unconscious if enough energy was gathered. But because the magic was so rare, the Sage who identified her magic could not determine what the Guardians' plan for her was. This made her both a celebrity among the villagers and an outcast among the other children. Despite this uncertainty, Marta had been developing her magic for the past six years and she feels that it has almost reached its maximum potential.

Nevertheless, even though she has abnormal (by Tel-ána standards) magic, that did not exempt her from doing the same chores that other children have, mainly gathering food and helping the grownups. Marta had an extra-vital job though. Twice a week, she would head up to Ricardo Castle, the center of the Iberian Kingdom's political and economic body, to receive supplies of meat, vegetables, and milk, food that they could not grow on their own, unlike fruit, wheat, and grain, which could be produced independently. Marta had an uncanny sense of direction. She knew precisely where on Tel-ána she was at any given time so knowing the route between the castle and her village was like knowing the back of her hand. The villagers trusted her with the bi-weekly delivery of the food even though there were some who had doubts that she was mature enough to handle such an essential task.

Marta was on her last run for the week. She was leading the horse-driven cart with food back to her village. As she crossed the bridge over the river that ran two-quarters around the area of land the village stood upon, she was unaware that somebody was observing her from the trees. The other two quarters of the small forest-bordered plateau her village stood upon wasn't even in their kingdom. Crossing the bridge meant she still had a quarter of daylight left, but this meant that she wouldn't get to her village until sunset. She believed she was making good time.

"Hi, Marta!" A voice called out. A boy around her age with light brown hair and green eyes dropped down from a tree into the cart and next to her.

Marta was startled, as was proven by her little gasp. "Daniel, I keep telling you to stop dropping in unexpectedly. One of these days, you'll make my heart stop."

"Aww, but all I wanted to do is see my most favorite cousin in the entire kingdom." Daniel laid his head on her left shoulder in a gesture of what appeared to be mock endearment to the casual observer.

"Oh for the love of the Guardians, I'm your only cousin in the kingdom. In fact, I'm your only cousin period." Daniel was the son of the brother of Marta's mother. His magic was called foresight. Despite the name, Daniel wasn't psychic; rather he had the ability to see through any matter and determine which sights were real and which were illusions. However, he was also a little bit of a prankster, especially when he would use his magic on a passing female.

"That only makes you all the more favorite to me," Daniel retorted.

"I doubt it."

"It's true!" Although neither of them would admit it openly, Marta and Daniel really did care about each other. They were close to the same age and lived near each other so they always played with one another and were very good friends. This sort of argument was just their way of saying hi. Everybody in the village knew that, but they allowed the two to continue their little charade, mostly because it was amusing. But as Marta and Daniel got older, they've gone through this comical routine less and less. Although, that didn't mean they would stop playing it altogether.

Marta shrugged his head off. Rolling her reddish-pink eyes, she commented, "You're such a child."

"Well you're no ancient one yourself," he countered.

"How did I get stuck with such a bizarre cousin?"

"The Guardians just love to play tricks on you, Marta."

Marta sighed, giving up this little war of cracks and put-downs. Trying to win a war of words with Daniel is like trying to walk without any legs, completely impossible.

As the wagon approached the village, Marta and Daniel could see smoke rise from the twenty or so houses that were enclosed within the ten-foot high wall. The mothers were already preparing pots and fires for cooking.

"Hey Marta, guess who's going for their lot test come next full moon." Daniel pointed to himself with his thumb while showing his usual smirking face. A lot test was held for children once they come of age (which for them would be sixteen years) and when the Sages believed that their powers have reached their pinnacle. The purpose of the lot test was to see which job would allow the person to use their magic efficiently to benefit the entire kingdom. Nobody is really sure what happens during the lot test except for the Sage performing the test and the person who actually takes the test. There has been lots of speculation among the candidates from sacrificing a baby goat to stripping naked and standing on hot coals.

Marta couldn't believe what she was hearing. Daniel was the same age as she was, yet if what he was saying was true (he may have been a prankster, but he was no liar); then he was already set to take his place as a working citizen of the Iberian Kingdom four years earlier than most of the other children their age, including her. He certainly didn't act like he was of age, with his ritual of startling her and his self-righteous attitude. "Don't tell me it's you."

"Yup, Sage Ben-Salaam came by while you were out. He said that he saw nobody maximize as fast as I." 'Maximize' was a term used for the development of a person's magic. Magic, like a person's body, develops as a person grows into adulthood and deteriorates as they become elderly.

"Yeah, I bet."

"No, really, he did say that."

"Hey, do you have a reason for coming out here other than to pester me?"

"Oh yeah, as a matter of fact, there was. Your mother told me to tell you to stop by your house first when you arrive. She needs to get the vegetables into the pot for the stew as soon as possible."

"Right, to my house it is." Daniel rode with Marta the rest of the way. Just like she predicted, the sun was descending into the horizon as she came into view of the guard bailey.

A platform ran along the inner part of the wall and encircled the whole village. It allowed guards to move around freely. The two guards who served as lookouts spotted Marta's wagon from their points. Marta waved to the guards.

"Good evening," Marta called.

"Good evening, Marta," one of the guards called back. He then looked at Daniel. "Daniel, are you sneaking up on your cousin again? Your mother's been looking for you." Daniel gulped. Sneaking out of the village close to nightfall was breaking the town's law of being inside the village by the time the sun goes down. This curfew was maintained simply because that in addition to bandits, there was pockets of "rogue magic," uncontrollable magic which could only be stopped by a Sage.

One of the guards called down to the handlers to open the door. With loud creaking, the door parted for the wagon. Once through, the doors were shut again. Even though there were only twenty huts (a total of fifteen families lived in the village), the village was pretty big. In addition to the houses, there was a park, a school, and a meeting tabernacle where the villagers would report their status to the Village Leader before the Leader would take off for the Iberian capitol to report the status of their village to the king.

Marta's house was towards the far end of the village. The roofs were made of a clay mixture and shaped to be curved to allow rain and snow to fall off of it. There were four extensions from the main room, two were bedrooms, one was a bathing room, and the other was a toilet. Marta's family did not own much, as did most families in the village, so there was never much crime. Daniel's family lived across the street and Daniel and Marta often had dinner at each other's house.

Daniel hopped down and went into his house where he would most likely be chewed out by his mother for sneaking out of the village so late in the afternoon. Marta carried a basket of vegetables into her house.

"Mother, I'm back," she called.

"Ooh, Marta, good, you're home. Please put the vegetables by the stove."

"I can't stay long. I still have to make the rest of the deliveries."

"Oh, don't worry; you will still have time, just drop the vegetables into the stove." Marta complied with her mother's wishes. As she returned to the wagon to make her rounds, her father came in.

"Good evening, Father," Marta greeted with a little bow. Her father simply nodded his head. Marta turned and went out to her wagon.

"I tell you, Asha, it's not right to trust such a vital task like delivering our food supply to a young girl like her."

"Oh, hush, Renaud," his mother scolded. "She's done such a good job so far, why spoil it for her? Besides, aren't you always the one who says she should contribute more to the village?"

Renaud just telekinetically lifted a glass to his spot at the table. Villagers found it hard to believe that such a cross and strict man could father such a usually cheerful and optimistic girl. Renaud wasn't afraid to pass strict judgment and even punishment on others, especially his own daughter. The two didn't even look alike, with Renaud having long black hair with streaks of gray on the sides and green eyes while Marta had short red hair and almost equally red eyes. Long hair was a sign of wisdom in Tel-ána, and especially the Iberian Kingdom. Marta, despite how she may act, was still considered a child by kingdom laws and, perhaps more importantly, her father's beliefs.

Marta performed the rest of her rounds to the village. The village adults were glad to see Marta and even gladder to see the food. The children said hi to her but other than that completely ignored her. One of the old women, someone who lived in the village all her life and only greeted visitors with two kisses, one on each cheek, gave Marta a few apples from the tree behind her hut. When Marta protested, the old woman oddly said, "We won't be around much longer to enjoy them anyway." Something about that comment gave Marta the shivers but gratefully accepted the apples.

When she and her family sat down, she noticed that her father seemed more uptight than usual. The old woman's cryptic message and her father's constant shifting of the eyes in her direction were making Marta apprehensive as well. Something was about to go down but Marta wasn't sure what, and she thought her father didn't know it as well.

Her mother could also sense the virtual hostility and sought to distract her family from it. "Marta, there's a full moon out tonight, so you know what that means..."

Marta moaned. "Oh great, bath night, can't I skip it this time?"

"You skipped it before," her mother reminded her. "Remember, you stunk for a week until Gregory pushed you into the river."

"But Daniel doesn't take a bath."

"How do you know he doesn't? Maybe he does."

"But Mom..."

"Marta, do as your mother commands," her father ordered more harshly than was prudent (in other words, his normal tone). Marta gave her father an annoyed look. "Don't look at me like that," he snapped.

"Like what?"

"I may not be a mind reader but I can tell when you're irritated at me, Marta and I don't like it, now stop acting childish like you always do." Now Marta's look changed to one of hurt. She wasn't trying to act childish; anybody could've seen that, anybody except her father.

Marta was reaching the limit of her patience with her father's constant pessimistic attitude. Normally she would just shrug it off or change the conversation but tonight she had enough. She decided to get right to the source of the problem. "Father, I do my part for the village, I follow your orders, do what you say, without expecting anything in return. Why can't you be satisfied with what I do?"

"When I think you've done something worthy of my appreciation, you will get it." Marta recoiled like she was tangibly slapped across the cheek.

Asha decided to take a stand. "Renaud, that'll be enough of that, your daughter is just looking for a little appreciation, why can't you give it to her?"

"Appreciation is like respect; it must be earned and not given."

"So what have you done to earn appreciation around here?" Asha retorted.

Renaud was about to reply when a loud whinny of a horse came from outside. Marta and her family got up and came out of their house.

A man in full armor stood at the open entrance to the village. The gold and silver dragon-shape crest on his shoulder showed that he was a knight from Ricardo Castle. It also showed that he was an important one. Any knight with silver and/or gold on their dragon crest was revealed to be very important to the king, which was why the village sentries immediately allowed him access to the village and were now standing on either side of the gate with confused looks on their faces.

"What would a royal knight be doing all the way out here?" Marta's mother asked. The other villagers came out of their houses and gathered around the knight. Marta saw Daniel standing on the other side of the knight. The two exchanged concerned glances, each thinking the same thing: what's this strange man doing here?

"Hear the words as dictated to me by King Gladirus, who lords over all of the Iberian Kingdom. He declares that you, the villagers of Gerard, send a representative to the village of Icthior, a full day's ride to the East of here, tomorrow to retrieve a very important package for the King and bring it back here. Once you return, a representative of the King will be here to accept your package."

"What business does the King wish here?" a villager asked.

"Silence, the King's orders are to be obeyed and not questioned! Now choose someone to go to Icthior tomorrow! Who will it be?" The King's orders had to be obeyed without reason. No matter how illogical the knight's request may seem, it had to be carried out.

Before even Marta could stop herself, she stepped forward. "I will. I will retrieve the package for the King." Marta didn't know why she was doing this. It wasn't that she didn't like King Gladirus; she never met him before and he rarely showed his face. Any official business was covered by either a messenger like the knight or one of his two Sages. Nobody in the outlying villages has gazed at his face and those who have are not talking.

She also didn't trust the knight. There was just something about him that gave her the willies. She never trusted any of the knights from Iberian Kingdom; mostly because of the way they look. They wore black and silver armor that covered all of their body, including their faces which made reading their facial expressions difficult. Who knows who or what they were underneath that armor. Not to mention the armor was coated by an elixir of the Sages that make them impervious to all types of magic. Their swords were also coated with the elixir. To be blunt, the only way to defeat an Iberian Knight is with swords, spears, and other bladed weapons. And the village barely had any of those melee weapons, let alone effective ones.

Some of the villagers inhaled sharply, clearly surprised by her action. Marta's virtual isolation over the obscurity of her magic made her rarely volunteer for anything, now she was stepping forward when everyone else was trying to do their best to avoid the knight looking in their direction. Her father, on the other hand, wasn't so much surprised as he was enraged. "Marta, what are you doing?"

"I know the area better than anyone," Marta said. "I know all the short cuts between the villages. I could get that package and be back by early the day after."

"She does know a lot about the area," one of the other villagers vouched.

"Very well," the knight said in an almost too willing voice. "You, child, shall be the retriever of the package for the king."

"Absolutely not!" Renaud shouted stepping forward. "I refuse to allow my daughter to undertake such a..." Renaud suddenly found himself staring at the business end of the knight's sword.

"Anybody who challenges the orders of the King will face my wrath. Do YOU challenge the will of the King?"

Grudgingly, Renaud shook his head. "It is not my intention to challenge the will of the King."

The knight withdrew his sword. "If I catch so much as a hint of betrayal from you, I will kill you where you stand, burn your body, and think nothing of it. You will wander the void for all eternity all because you opposed the king. Do I make myself clear?"

"Yes, sir."

Marta settled her body into the large tub of water that night. As usual, it was hot to the boiling point thanks to Asha's magic but Marta was tough, she could withstand it.

"I can't believe you agreed to do such a task, Marta, such a move is very out of character for you," her mother said tossing her a washing cloth and soap.

"Mom, I'm just going to retrieve and deliver a package," Marta protested as she lathered some soap onto the cloth. "It's not like I'm going off to kill a Sage or something."

"But didn't you tell me once that you don't trust anybody who works directly under the king?"

Marta, who was in the middle of rubbing the soapy cloth on her body, paused. "Yeah, I did…" Of course, that was three years ago.

"So why do you want to do that favor for the king?"

"Why are you making such a big deal, Mom?" Marta asked. "It's just delivering one little package. Don't you have any faith in me?"

"You're right, dear, I'm sorry. Lean forward." Marta moved onto her knees and tilted her upper body downward so that her mother could wash her back. "To tell you the truth, I'm proud of you for choosing to undertake this task. It shows that you are willing to look beyond your personal beliefs for the good of the kingdom."

"Thanks, Mom." Marta's tone dropped a few octaves as she continued in a depressed timbre. "I just wish that Father had as much confidence in me as you have."

"Your father is very proud of you, Marta. He just shows it in his… unusual way."

"Very unusual," Marta added.

"Under." Marta, closed her eyes, held her breath, and plugged her nose. She lowered her entire head under the water.

"Marta, someday I hope you understand how much your father loves you and how much he's willing to go through just to make you happy." It was too bad Marta was under water otherwise she would've heard and took comfort in her mother's plea. When Marta surfaced, her mother handed her a towel and told her to get ready for bed.

As soon as Marta was asleep, Asha turned to exit the house. As she passed Renaud, who was writing a letter, she said, "Your daughter shows much maturity, more so than you I might add. Are you sure this is wise?"

"In the long terms, yes," Renaud replied.

"That's what I was afraid you would say." She continued her way out and went across the street. One of the houses across the street had a lit window and Asha stood by it. "Marta leaves mid-morning tomorrow," she said. To the casual observer, it looked like she was talking to no one but in fact she was talking to somebody, a boy inside the lit room. "Something is wrong, please watch out for her."

The next day, Marta set out on her wagon to the village of Icthior.

"I don't believe this," she muttered to herself. "Mother is right, I don't trust the King; I definitely don't trust that knight, what made me decide to do this?"

"That's what I want to know." Marta screamed and almost jumped out of her clothes as a familiar voice came from the back of her wagon. Daniel poked his head up from underneath the hay that was normally laid there to keep the food crates from colliding with one another. "Hello."

"For crying out loud, Daniel, what are you doing there? Does your mother know you're doing this?"

"No, but yours does. She was the one who suggested I do this to begin with, to keep an eye on you."

"So she really does have no faith in me," Marta said more to herself than to Daniel as she remembered the conversation she had with her the night before.

"It's not that your mother doesn't have any faith in you, Marta, it's just that she doesn't have any faith is our surroundings. There are all sorts of wild animals, bandits, and rogue magic around. It's better to travel in company."

"Yeah, yeah, yeah," Marta said as if she didn't want to hear about the dangers the forest presented. But truthfully, she was glad that Daniel was along for the ride. At least if anything bad happens, she would have him to back her up even though his magic was relatively weak. Marta started to wonder if Daniel's childish façade was just that.

It was late afternoon by the time the Icthior skyline became visible. Icthior was a tree-based village. The ground wasn't firm enough to support houses and other structures so many of the houses were in trees, connected by a series of rope bridges and plank walkways. However, it did have an outer wall and door like Gerard.

"Hello!" Marta called. There was a moment of pause before a sentry stuck his head out from over the outer wall. The sentry's armor was shaped in similar style to the armor that Gerard's gatekeepers wore but the color was vastly different, green and brown to blend in with the surroundings.

"Who goes there? Identify yourself!" The sentry demanded.

"I am Marta, this is my cousin Daniel," Marta introduced. "We come from the village of Gerard. We have come to pick up the package."

"What package?" The guard questioned.

Marta and Daniel exchanged a look before Daniel spoke up, "We were told there would be a package for the King of the Iberian Kingdom."

"Stay right there," the guard commanded. He disappeared from view. Minutes later, the doors opened. A small wooden elevator built into a tree was lowered and an elderly man came out onto a wooden platform in front of the doorway. His eyes had a deep blue glow to them.

"My name is Bishcott," he greeted as the elevator was raised back into the trees. "I am the chief of this village. What is this you say of a package?"

"A royal knight came to us yesterday and told us that there would be a package here for him. He asked us to pick it up for him," Marta informed him as she and Daniel hopped off the wagon.

"There must be some mistake," Bishcott said. "We have no package, nor were we told that someone would be here to pick up a package. Are you sure you have the right village?"

"This is the village of Icthior, is it not?" Daniel asked.

"It is."

"Well the knight told us that there will be a package for the king waiting in Icthior. He asked us to go retrieve it."

"It is like I said, we have no package nor did someone hand us a package for the king," Bishcott repeated.

"But that doesn't make any sense," Daniel said. "Maybe he got the village wrong."

"My magic is truth sight, meaning I can tell if someone is telling the truth or not. I know you are not lying, but perhaps the knight was."

"Maybe, but…"

"Chief Bishcott!" A woman with silver hair and fine skin with a bandage around her eyes came down on the elevator being escorted by a child.

"It is our Oracle," Bishcott identified. Marta and Daniel gasped. Oracles were very rare in Tel-ána. Very few villages had them. They could tell the future but at a great price, their eyesight magically locked by the Sages to allow the Guardians to show them visions of the future. Their birth names, their very identities, also had to be sacrificed. There were only about fifteen known Oracles in all of Tel-ána. They were reveled almost as much as Sages were.

"Chief Bishcott, something horrible has happened! A village has been attacked."

Daniel began to get a bad feeling. It was like a big warning sound went off in his head. Even before the Oracle gave the specifics, he knew what happened.

"What village, Oracle?"

"The village of Gerard."

Marta's reaction was of pure shock. So was Daniel, even though his gut warned him ahead of time.

"We must return to the village," Marta said.

"We would never make it there before nightfall," Daniel came back.

"Perhaps we can help you," Chief Bishcott said and turned to the child that brought Oracle out. "Lad, go get Vernard and bring him here."

"Yes, Chief." In no time at all, an overly muscular man arrived at them.

"Vernard can supplement the talents of any natural life form as long as he's in direct contact with it," Bishcott explained. "He will give your horse enhanced speed to bring you back to your village."

"Right."

True to Bishcott's word, Marta and Daniel reached Gerard in less than half the time it took them to get from there to Icthior thanks to Vernard.

The bridge still seemed to be intact but as they got to the general area of Gerard, they saw a large black column of smoke coming out from the vicinity of the town. Marta leaped off the wagon and ran the rest of the way. When she got to the wall, she stopped short. The large door was off its hinges, leaning at a diagonal angle blocking their way into the village along with the accompanying debris.

Daniel and Vernard caught up with her.

"The Oracle was right," Daniel said solemnly. "Gerard was attacked." But why, did the knight decide to destroy the village because Marta's father was being cross? For that matter, did the knight do it at all?

Marta began moving her body in a series of strange gestures. Daniel knew what was happening. Marta was going to use her magic. She was already beginning her dance, gathering the energies around her for a vibro-shock. She first rotated her left arm in a clockwise movement. She then brought her right arm over her left arm on her left side. After repeating the process on her right side, she then crossed both arms at her center and spread them out. She then moved them in another clockwise rotation. She repeated this process a couple of times.

"Watch out," Daniel warned, knowing how powerful Marta could make her vibro-shocks. He grabbed Vernard and they dove behind a tree.

Marta was finished with her dance. Her hands were clenched at her side in a cup formation. They were shaking, but not from the energy she gathered.

"Vibro-shock." Marta whispered forcing her arms out, palms open. The soft cry was a focus point for her. It helped her concentrate her magic and even increased them a little. The air seemed to waver and the door burst into splinters.

When the smoke and woodchips cleared, they could see the inside of the village. Most of the houses there had collapsed and those that had not were burning. As they entered, they saw dead animals stacked up, unfit for even consumption. Daniel looked to his left and screamed. Marta and Vernard followed and let out audible gasps of their own. The guards' naked bodies were impaled on wooden pikes.

"The calling sign of bandits," Vernard muttered. "They did this as a warning not to mess with them."

"But a warning to whom?" Daniel asked.

Marta ran down the street and discovered that her house was one of the lucky ones. A giant hole was in the roof but the walls were still standing.

"Mother, Father," Marta cried out. "Mother, please, answer me! Father, where are you?" Silence answered her. Daniel decided to use his own magic. His eyes turned from their normal brown to an indigo blue. He saw outlines of the rubble and walls. But he could find no bodies. He placed a hand on Marta's shoulder and although she didn't turn around, she knew he was shaking his head.

Marta couldn't contain her sorrow anymore. She had been holding back tears in hope that somebody, anybody, would've survived. She held that hope all the way from Icthior. Now she realizes that it was a pointless wish and saw no reason to hold back any more. She collapsed to her knees sobbing, tears pouring from her eyes. Daniel, in a movement out of his normal character, embraced her from behind. Vernard just stood behind them, shock registering in his eyes.

Nighttime had descended on the Iberian Kingdom. The full moon once again cast its glow onto the kingdom, more specifically the small tree village of Icthior. Some people would find it breathtakingly beautiful while others would simply find it an annoyance.

Daniel was one of the people who thought it was an annoyance because it didn't reflect his mood. At the moment, his mood was dark. Gerard, the village he lived in all his life, had been destroyed. His entire family, all his friends, everyone, they have all been killed by some unknown enemy... was it unknown? Daniel's instinct started to tell him something but he refused to admit it. Then again, it was this same feeling that also warned him that something bad happened to Gerard.

At the moment, Daniel was in the wooden meeting hut at the nexus of the labyrinth-like tree village talking with Vernard and

Chief Bishcott. Marta had cried herself to sleep all the way back to Icthior and nobody saw the need to wake her.

"Believe me, Chief Bishcott, I wouldn't have believed it had I not seen it with my own eyes," Vernard said, finishing his account of what was discovered at Gerard's remains.

"An entire village destroyed..." Bishcott shook his head. "Even if the culprits all had incredible devastating magic, only an army could've done so much destruction in such a short amount of time."

"But there's no way a foreign army could've gotten past our kingdom's sentry outposts," Daniel protested.

"Perhaps they were already inside the kingdom and were waiting for the right time to strike," Vernard suggested.

Chief Bishcott's abnormally blue eyes glowed. "Or perhaps it was an inside job."

"You've got to be kidding, Chief Bishcott, why would the Iberian Army destroy a village, especially considering the village was out of the way from most of the other villages and no strategic value?" Vernard argued.

"Not to mention that it was a village in their own kingdom," Daniel added.

"Chief Bishcott," a villager called from outside. "Straos has returned."

"Send him in," Bishcott ordered. Straos was a flyer who was sent on recon not long after Marta, Daniel, and Vernard returned to Icthior.

Straos came in and got down on one knee. "Chief Bishcott, I flew over the former Gerard area. I could find nobody, but I did find this." Straos held out a gold and silver dragon-shaped crest.

"I was afraid of that; that is a crest of an Iberian knight."

Daniel slammed his hand on the table; this only confirmed what his instinct revealed to him earlier. "I can't believe it; my own King destroyed our village."

"That is a logical conclusion," Chief Bishcott agreed. "But is it the correct one?" Nobody had an answer to that.

"So what are we going to do about it?" Vernard asked.

"I'll tell you what we're going to do!" It was Marta. She was on one knee on the mat Chief Bishcott had laid out for her. Her head was lowered but as she raised her head, everyone could see that her eyes were bloodshot and from the look of it, it wasn't from the lack of sleep. "We're going to Ricardo Castle and make King Gladirus pay severely for what he did!"

The four males stared horribly at Marta's attitude, especially Daniel. He had never seen his cousin so bloodthirsty before. She normally didn't like to fight, let alone murder someone. "Marta, are you insane? We can't challenge King Gladirus. He'd put us to death before we even reached the inner palace."

"I don't care if the Guardians themselves intervene, I will make him pay for destroying my village!"

"Might I suggest a compromise?" Chief Bishcott suggested. "Why don't you request an audience with King Gladirus? Once you have it, ask his reasoning behind the destruction of the village. Being the righteous individual that he is, King Gladirus will provide you with a full and detailed response. After that, you two can decide what to do next."

"What's there to reason?" Marta came back. "He ordered the destruction of our village. We must avenge their destruction!"

"Marta, I agree with Chief Bishcott on this one," Daniel voiced.

"But Daniel, you must want to avenge your family... our family as much as I do!"

"Yes, I do, but going in there with rage is no way to get any answers. Besides, how do we know King Gladirus really authorized the attack? Perhaps it is some sort of a prelude to an overthrow by the army; perhaps one of the other kingdoms' armies dressed up in Iberian armor and masqueraded their way into the village. We won't know for sure unless we ask. Marta, I know this is odd for me to say, but let's wait, let's find out the truth before getting revenge."

Marta sighed. She was still levelheaded enough to know when she had been out voted. "Very well, we'll go ask him, though I hardly see the point."

"We shall give you cloaks with our symbols on them," Bishcott offered. "That way, if you run across any knights, they won't connect you with the Gerard disaster."

"Okay," Daniel and Marta said at the same time.

The next morning, Daniel and Marta were outfitted with cloaks bearing the green triangle of Icthior village. They were given enough supplies to last them a few days.

Chief Bishcott gave them one last instruction. "If you travel to Ricardo Castle via the Nacorian Valley near the Temple of Maran, you'll be able to bypass most of the guard checkpoints, but even if you come across one of the royal knights, you know what to say."

"We're travelers from Icthior coming to see our parents in Ricardo Castle," Marta recited.

"Good luck, children." Marta and Daniel mounted their horses and took off.

Chief Bishcott watched them leave along with Vernard and Oracle.

"My Chief, are you sure it is wise to send them on such a dangerous mission?" Vernard asked.

"I don't feel it's wise, Vernard, but I do feel that it's necessary. Besides, if what I am sensing is true, then those children might be the only thing standing between purity... and corruption."

Ricardo Castle was stationed on top of a cliff overlooking the eastern region of the Iberian Kingdom. Named for the warrior who first claimed the territory that was going to become the Iberian Kingdom and his five descendants, the castle was put there on purpose so that it would be the first thing the sun sees when it rises and the last thing it sees when it sets. While the castle itself was on top of the cliff, the town that accompanied the kingdom was situated on the opposite side of the chasm. Because the bluff the castle stood on was higher than the one the village was on, a method was devised by the early Iberian Sages to get up there with ease. However, that method was only known to the nobility who lived in Ricardo Castle. Everybody else was kept in the dark to keep from any of the other kingdoms in Tel-ána from finding out and staging an all out assault on the castle.

King Gladirus stood on a balcony that overlooked the Iberian Capital; his grizzly features showed that something was disturbing him. His Sage, Mattonda Giersi, had told him that one of the villages on the Iberian boarder had defected to the neighboring kingdom of Morbia and were now plotting an overthrow of the king. He didn't understand why. He tried to be a staunch and fair ruler, but as his father told him on his deathbed, no one king shall ever have his subjects fully under control.

"Sage," Gladirus called. Immediately, Sage Mattonda was at his side. Like all Sages, Mattonda was dressed in purple robes with an exotic headdress covering his midnight blue hair. He wore a talisman around his neck, a cross with crescents on all ends that made it look like a circle. He carried a silver staff with a purple orb on one end.

"I am at your service, Your Highness."

"Please tell me the truth; has the rebellion been put down?"

"Fortunately it has, Your Highness, I sent three of our best platoons to deal with it. Unfortunately there was… bloodshed."

Gladirus cursed mentally. "The things I must do to retain peace around here."

"Do not blame yourself, Your Highness. Some people will never be satisfied with what they have."

Gladirus smiled. "Thank you, old friend. You do not know how comforting your words are."

"I live only to serve the king." As Mattonda turned to leave, he scowled at Gladirus' back. The fool, he thought, he has no idea of the trouble he's about to unleash on himself.

Marta and Daniel galloped through the forest on the horses they obtained from Icthior Village.

"Marta," Daniel called back to her. "Do you really think King Gladirus had a hand in destroying our village? I find it hard to believe. There's no rhyme or reason to do such a reckless and spiteful act."

"Are you crazy?" Marta asked her cousin. "That crest that we found was from one of Iberian's soldiers. What more proof do you need?"

"I don't know; something's just abnormal about this. Things like this are rarely that simple."

"Well once we corner King Gladirus, we'll force the information out of him." Daniel was worried about his cousin's aggressive attitude. Don't get him wrong, he was just as anxious to avenge their village as she was, if not more so, but something didn't add up here. He hoped it was just him being paranoid.

Then again, it was his paranoia that first told him that something bad had happened to Gerard.

Marta pulled up to Daniel then passed him. "Hey, Marta, wait up!" Daniel called accelerating his horse to catch up to Marta's. Suddenly his horse tripped spilling both of them onto the ground

"Daniel!" Marta brought her horse to a halt then jumped off. She helped him to his feet. "Are you all right?"

"I think so, but what made my horse trip like that." Marta and Daniel looked behind them to see several branches writhing like snakes. "Those tree roots, they're alive!" The tree roots leaped towards them. Marta and Daniel tried to run away but the live tree roots were much faster than they were. In no time at all, they were wrapped up in their grasp.

"Is this rogue magic?" Daniel asked between grunts of pain.

"I don't know, but they're dead!" Marta began moving her hands in alternating circular movements. Because she was tied up, she would only be able to gather the terrestrial energies within her organic cocoon. Her vibro-shock blast would not have as much power as it usually does, but maybe it will have enough to free her arms so she could perform a larger vibro-shock. She only hoped she had enough time. Marta released what energy she gathered. The tree roots bulged and loosened. Marta dropped to the ground and began moving her entire body in a rhythmic movement. Marta kept doing her dance for almost a minute. With a loud audio cry of her magic's title, she released the energy she gathered through her dance. The tree roots holding Daniel were destroyed and his body crumbled to the ground.

"Daniel!" Marta rushed over to him to search for signs of life. He had fallen unconscious but he was still breathing. "Hang on, cousin, I've got you." Marta looked around and spotted a large stone structure in the distance. Leaving their horses, she dragged Daniel towards the structure.

When Daniel came to, he was in a dark room surrounded by stone walls. All sorts of strange carvings were on the walls. A fire was mutely glowing in the center. Marta fell asleep sitting up, her knees pulled up against her chest, the cloak Chief Bishcott of Icthior Village gave her covering her body. Daniel got up and gently shook Marta awake. "Marta?"

Marta opened her light pink eyes and looked up at him. "Daniel, oh good, you're awake." She sounded relieved as she hugged him. Daniel was surprised and secretly pleased. Was this the bloodthirsty girl he was talking to not long ago? Daniel always loved Marta's optimism and energy, in other words how she was before Gerard was destroyed.

"Marta, where are we?"

"It's the Temple of Maran."

"The Temple of Maran? Marta, we're not here to sightsee, we need to get to Ricardo Castle."

"Daniel, you've been unconscious all day. If we were to leave now, we would get into all sorts of trouble. You said it yourself that wild animals and bandits often roam around looking for people to terrorize. And let's not forget rogue magic like those tree roots that knocked you out in the first place."

"What do you mean by all day, Marta?" Marta pointed to something behind Daniel. He turned around and saw the exit. Outside was the forest, bathed in the moonlight.

"After the attack, I quickly took us to here to escape the live tree roots. There's seems to be a special mist around this temple that prevents intruders from using their magic. I already tried my vibro-shock and it failed."

"Oh, I see. So what do we do now?"

"We might as well look around. Perhaps there's a back entrance. If not, we'll have to wait until morning."

"Oh, fine." Marta lit a torch with one of the crystals she used to make the campfire and together they dove deeper into the temple. The temple was a labyrinth of caverns. At one of many intersections, there was some writing.

"Marta, what is this? I don't recognize the writing."

"Nor do I." Marta touched the writing and it began to glow. She dropped the torch and it went out as her pupils disappeared for a minute.

"Marta?" Marta didn't respond. "Marta, you're scaring me. Marta?"

"This is the Temple of Maran," Marta stated as if in a trance. "Long ago, this served as a burial tomb for an unknown body. It is said that the soul of that body still roams free, searching for an identity."

Marta's eyes returned to their normal status. Daniel stared at his cousin, not believing what he just heard. Marta just told him the entire story of the Temple of Maran and he knew she didn't even know it this morning. As far as people of Tel-ána, and especially the citizens of the Iberian Kingdom, were concerned, the Temple of Maran was nothing more than a tourist attraction, a tribute to Tel-ána's ancient history. The temple itself was actually built into a cliff wall. Marta and Daniel didn't know if others had had similar experiences or if they were the first.

Suddenly Daniel felt a familiar tingling in his eyes, a tingle that everyone on Tel-ána associated with the existence and function of one's own magic. "Marta, my foresight is working."

"You're kidding, how?"

"I'm not exactly sure. The only reason I can think of is that the only type of magic not affected by the mist is magic that can activate from outside the human body."

"Use it, see if there's another passage way." Daniel nodded. His eyes turned blue on the outside. On the inside, it was like everything was in white outline. He looked around and saw that there were a series of lines to their right. Returning to his normal vision, he saw a wall where the passageway should be. Daniel went over to the wall and felt along it until his hand slid into a panel. An entire section of the wall rotated 90 degrees. Through the wall was a passageway lit by torches.

"Good job, cousin," Marta congratulated. Taking one of the torches from its holder, Marta and Daniel crept down the passageway, the passageway that was giving them the creeps.

"Hey, do you hear that?" Daniel asked.

"Probably just my heart beating faster and faster," Marta commented trying to ease their obvious fright.

"No, it's something else." Daniel activated his foresight vision again and looked around but he couldn't see anything.

Finally, Marta and Daniel came to a dead end, or so they thought. Just like the first one, the wall rotated to allow them entrance. Inside was what looked like a crypt.

A stone container was at the other end.

"A… a tomb," Daniel stuttered.

"Well it makes sense," Marta said placing the torch on a holder near the entrance. "Remember what the scripture said, this place was originally a burial tomb."

"Yeah, remember what else the scripture said? It said that the soul of the body that was buried here still roams free."

"It… it's probably just a rumor, a legend meant to scare out grave robbers," Marta said with a lot less confidence than her face showed. Marta and Daniel went up to the crypt. They could hear the sound of wind blowing but couldn't feel it. "P… perhaps we should turn back."

"Yeah, I agree." But as Marta and Daniel turned around to leave, the wall rotated again, locking them in. The two let out a scream before Daniel said, "Oh no, we're trapped here, probably forever!"

A rumbling came from the crypt. Marta and Daniel turned as one and looked at it. They looked at each other, each asking the other permission for something they both did not want to do: open the crypt. They pushed the top of the crypt to the side. It fell off and shattered into pieces.

Inside, buried underneath what seemed like centuries of dust was a small human skeleton. It was dressed in a blue tunic and red leggings. Its head, originally facing straight up, fell to one side from the small wind generated by the moving of the cover. Daniel and Marta screamed at the top of their lungs and quickly backed away.

"That was a bad idea," Daniel commented panting heavily.

"No kidding," Marta agreed, her breathing echoing his. "What else could happen?" Blue smoke began rising from the crypt. "Something tells me I shouldn't have asked that."

The smoke quickly turned into blue light and then energy. Daniel and Marta covered their eyes. When they opened them again, they saw a figure. He looked like a young boy, probably around 8 or 9. He had wavy hair and his eyes looked distant. He was transparent and had a light blue outline and had no legs.

Marta and Daniel grabbed one another in fright and screamed at the top of their lungs again but this time there were words accompanying it. "IT'S A GHOST!"

"Wait, please, don't be afraid," the ghost pleaded approaching them. "I won't hurt you." But Marta and Daniel were afraid, very afraid. Marta got ready to release her vibro-shock when she remembered that she couldn't use it.

"Stay away," Marta warned. "Just because I can't use my magic doesn't mean I can't fight." She swung her arms at the ghost but passed right through him. Not giving up, Marta lunged at the small ghost but only ended up landing on the crypt. She came face-to-face with the skeleton's head. Marta screamed and rolled off the casket.

"Please, be calm, I will not hurt you. I couldn't even if I wanted to. You can see why."

"Who are you?" Daniel asked finding his voice.

The ghost boy lowered his head. "I... I don't know my name," he said in a shamed voice.

"Well, what do you call yourself?" Marta asked.

"I... don't call myself anything, had no need to."

"You mean you haven't revealed yourself to anybody else?"

"You're the first that has ever visited this chamber."

"Then that must be your body?" Marta looked down at the skeleton in the crypt.

"I guess so. I seem to be anchored to this crypt. I can't leave this chamber or the surrounding area. Please, tell me where I am?"

"It's the Temple of Maran in the Iberian Kingdom. Have you heard of it?" Daniel asked.

The boy shook his head. "No, all I know is that I've been stuck here for as long as I can remember." The boy seemed depressed, and who could blame him? He had no clue as to who he was or how he died. He probably hasn't even been outside. He was, in all respects, an outcast. Marta's heart went out to him.

Something caught her eye. She looked down and saw something shining just under the body's right hand. She edged the hand off and picked it up. It was a crystal, a prism about the size of her index finger. A loop was carved onto the end of it. It was shining the same color as the ghost. "Hey Daniel, look at this." Daniel and the ghost stared at it. Marta held it next to the ghost boy and the light increased almost blindly. "Um... Ghost, do you know what this is?"

"No, but... it feels important, like it's the key to my existence."

"It's possible that this is what's keeping you from leaving the chamber," Daniel deduced.

"It might even explain why you're here and not in the Guardians' Dimension.

The boy smiled, hopeful glint in his eye. "Yes... yes, you might be right."

"Hey, I know, why don't you come with us?" Daniel offered as Marta slipped the crystal's loop around her neck. "We're on our way to Ricardo Castle, the capital of the Iberian Kingdom."

"For a chance to leave this room and see something new, I don't care what the end point is. But are you sure you want me along, I mean I don't want to be a bother."

"Hey, don't worry about it. If I can handle Daniel, I can handle anyone."

"Hey!"

"Besides, we might find out some more about you... hmm, you need a name."

"Well, we found him at the Temple of Maran," Daniel said. He turned to the ghost. "So for now, why don't we call you Maran?"

"Maran..." The ghost said the name a couple of times before he decided, "Yeah, I like that. From now on, I'm Maran."

"Then welcome aboard, Maran." Marta held out her hand. Daniel put his on top of hers. Maran tried placing his hand on top but ended up passing it right through their hands. All three of them smiled.

"So... how do we get out of here?" Daniel asked, the tender moment ended.

"Maybe like this," Maran said and floated right through the wall. A couple of seconds later, he floated back, "Are you coming?"

"We can't do that," Daniel protested.

"Why not?"

"We're not ghosts."

"Daniel, how did you open the door the first time?"

"Let's see..." Daniel once again slid his hand along the wall and ended up touching a brick perpendicular to his stomach. The wall turned and Daniel and Marta ran through fearing the door would close and locked them in again. They made it back to the hallway. "Now I'm lost, which way did we come from?"

"This is strange," Maran commented flying along the wall. "I know I've traveled these hallways before, but it's like I'm looking at them for the first time."

"Daniel, do you smell that?"

"Yeah, smells like smoke."

"Come on, if that's what I think it is..." The three followed the trail, pausing just long enough to show Maran the scripture warning. Maran couldn't read it and could only pass his hand through the wall. Finally, they returned to their campfire. Maran was entranced by the fire. Marta and Daniel reached the conclusion that stone and cement were the only things Maran had seen up to this point.

"Let's get some sleep. We have a long journey ahead of us."

The next morning, Marta and Daniel left the temple with Maran in tow. The crystal that seemed to contain Maran's very spirit was still wrapped around Marta's neck.

Maran stared up at the bright sunlight. "Wow, that's bright."

"Yeah, it is," Daniel agreed shielding his eyes.

"Maran, have you ever been outside before?"

"Not to my knowledge."

"Talk about being kept in the dark," Daniel cracked.

"Daniel!" Daniel at first thought Marta was groaning at his joke, and then he looked in her direction and spotted the living tree roots waving in front of them, blocking their passage.

"Oh great, these things again; what are we going to do?"

Maran looked around. "Marta, I don't think these vines are natural," he said calmly.

"You think so?" Daniel asked sarcastically as he tried to fend them off with a stick.

"Yes, someone is deliberately causing this."

"Are you sure?" Marta asked.

"I don't know how I know, I guess it's something inside of me, but yes this is definitely the work of someone."

"Find him," Marta ordered. Maran rose into the treetops. After a while, there was a loud scream as someone fell to the ground. The vines descended back into the ground.

"What did you do?" Daniel asked Maran.

"I don't know, I just appeared in front of him and he panicked."

"It's a good thing you came with us after all," Daniel commented. Marta went over and picked up the figure. It was a boy a little older than them. He had scraggly dark hair and a scar over one eye, the other was a deep brown. He was dressed in a green shirt and leggings. A dagger was sheathed in his left boot. She held him by the collar of his shirt.

"Why did you attack us?" Marta asked. "Who are you?

The boy smirked. "I'm just an ordinary thief who's about to rob you of all your belongings."

Suddenly tree roots sprouted up from under Marta and Daniel and grabbed them by their legs. They also tried to grab Maran but only passed right through him.

"I have been waiting for you since yesterday. My vines couldn't penetrate the temple walls, but now that you have left its sanctuary, I can get all your belongings, maybe even the clothes off your back." The thief smiled lewdly.

"That's what you think," Marta said as she begun her vibro dance. She gathered enough energy and hurled it at the thief calling out, "Vibro-shock!" The thief went down but managed to get up to one knee. As Marta came close, he reached to his boot and the dagger that was in it.

"Marta, look out!" Maran cried as he flew forward. He actually went right into the thief's mouth. The thief, as a result, was thrown back.

"Maran," Marta and Daniel both cried out. Marta ran up to the thief and gripped him by the collar of his shirt. "All right, you maniac, what did you do to Maran?"

The thief opened his good eye, but there was something different about him. He seemed more relax and not as malicious. "Marta."

"Huh?" His voice, it was much softer. In fact, it almost sounded like… "Maran, is that you?"

"Yes. Somehow I have gained control of this boy's body."

"Daniel, could you use your foresight to find out if that's really Maran in there," Marta instructed. Daniel's eyes turned blue. He could see an outline of the thief but what filled that body was Maran's outline.

"He's right; that is Maran inside." The cousins couldn't believe it; somehow, being a ghost must grant Maran the ability to control other people by going inside them.

Maran tried to walk, but he was behaving like a drunk, staggering from right to left. Marta and Daniel each grabbed one of Maran's hands and began to lead him along.

It was mid afternoon when Marta, Daniel, and Maran arrived at a hilltop. By then, Maran had gotten the hang of walking (the last mile or so, he only fell down three times). Down below them was the Iberian capital.

"There it is," Daniel said. "Just across the bridge is Ricardo Castle where we will find King Gladirus."

"Yes," Marta agreed harshly. "And then we will make him pay for destroying our village."

"Marta, we are not here for revenge," Daniel reminded her. "We are just here to find out the truth. Maybe King Gladirus didn't authorize such an action."

"No, Daniel, I refuse to believe that. King Gladirus deliberately destroyed our village, he had to."

"But why, why would he do this?"

"Who cares why he did that, the point is he did and now he must pay."

"Perhaps we should wait until morning to..." Maran was interrupted as a convulsion raked through his host's body.

"Maran, what's wrong?" Marta asked, worried for her new friend.

"I... don't... know! I feel like... I'm losing control!" Maran was ejected from the thief's body. Marta and Daniel immediately went over to Maran.

"Maran, are you all right?" Daniel said offering his hand.

"I feel weary," Maran reported. "But other than that, I'm fine."

The thief was coming around. "Where am I?" He groaned. He then saw the city. "By the Guardians, I just escaped from here the other day! I don't want to go back! Wait a second, how did I get back here?"

"Our ghost friend here took control of you," Daniel explained.

"Hey you, thief boy," Marta said harshly grabbing the thief by his collar. "You said you escaped from here. Can I assume it was from the castle dungeon?" The thief nodded. "Then perhaps you can show us the way in."

"Are you crazy, girl? You WANT to get captured?"

"I want... to kill King Gladirus!"

"Now I know you're crazy. I'm a thief, not a murderer. I'm out of here."

"You'll show us the way or I will use my magic to give you a few more scars."

"Sorry, girlie, but it'll take more than that to convince me to do such an act."

"Perhaps I can find out by going inside him again," Maran volunteered. He got ready to insert himself into the thief's body.

"Wait, wait," the thief amended. Apparently, getting possessed again didn't appeal to him. "I'll show you how I escaped but that's it. I won't take part in this hair-brained scheme."

"Good enough," Marta declared. She dropped him.

"Boy, you have a strong grip for a little girl," the thief commented.

"My name is Marta. That's my cousin Daniel and our ghost friend is Maran. Do you have a name?"

The thief paused for a minute, afraid to tell them his real name. He has wanted to get rid of his past, and changing his name might be a good way to start. He thought about an alias he could use and finally, he answered, "Just call me Andros."

Maran tilted his head to one side. It didn't sound like his real name but Maran was willing to give him the benefit of a doubt. Besides, he was hardly one to judge names, considering how he doesn't even know what his own name is. "Okay, Andros."

"Well, Marta, Daniel, and Maran, follow me." Andros began to lead them into the city.

The city was a bunch of sand rock buildings stacked upon one another and closely packed together, so packed, that the shops were also citizens' homes. A main street led to the bridge across the chasm.

Andros pulled Marta and Daniel into an alley. He reached into his tunic and pulled out an eye patch. He fitted it over his scarred eye then pulled up a hood that was tucked into the tunic. Maran asked what he was doing.

"The guards will recognize me by my scar," the thief explained. "This way, they can't be sure that it is me."

"Why would you need to…?" Daniel's question was interrupted by the sight of two knights at the city end of the bridge. They aimed their enchanted spears at the group.

"No one shall pass," one of the guards declared. Maran quickly hid behind Daniel.

"That's okay," the thief said. "It is not our intention to pass; I merely wanted to show my siblings the castle. We'll stay on this side if it makes you feel better."

The knights looked at each other and stood down. The thief led Daniel and Marta to a small lookout to the left of the bridge. He pretended to point at the castle but instead pointed to below the bridge where a sewer grate was embedded into the cliff wall.

"You see that grate down there? Well it leads right up to the dungeon. The current's pretty strong though. I had to stop myself several times from flying out."

"I'm sure if we hold on to the walls, we'll be able to stop ourselves," Marta commented.

"Wait a minute," Daniel said. "Why do we have to sneak in when we can just request an audience?"

"It could take too long waiting for a reply," Marta answered. "We need to strike now while he's unguarded."

"No, Marta, I thought we agreed just to find out information, not for revenge."

"You gather information; I'll get in there and use my magic to clobber King Gladirus from here to Darinka!"

"Perhaps we should wait until tomorrow to decide how we should approach this," Maran suggested.

"Spirit boy has a good idea," Andros agreed. "Even if you were to choose the revenge angle, it would take a while to travel the sewers. Tell you what, we'll find a room for the night, and then we'll set out to the castle tomorrow morning."

"Fine," Marta grumbled.

"Um… one question, how are we going to get a room? We don't have a lot of money."

The thief reached into his pouch and pulled out a small metal pick. "Let's just say I'm a jack of all trades."

The four got into a room at a tavern by having the Andros pick the lock to a window. The ledge the window was on was perfectly adjacent to the roof of another building so it didn't require much balance. Marta and Daniel got the two beds while the thief camped out on the floor. Maran just hovered there. He really didn't feel the need to sleep, probably because he was already asleep. However, half-way through the night, he decided he should at least make the illusion of sleeping so he curled up under Marta's bed and drifted into his own private world, imagining different scenarios as to who he was and how he died.

Marta woke up before anyone else. Daniel and the thief were still asleep and Maran was nowhere to be seen. Marta got up and silently went to the washroom. As she filled a basin of cold water, she ran over her plan again. She would knock out the guards who were stationed at the bridge with her magic, then sneak in through the sewer grate. She would find King Gladirus, hopefully at his most vulnerable time, and then using the thief's dagger, she would strike.

Marta washed her face and gazed into her reflection in the water. She thought back to the old days. Normally, she would already be heading for the capitol to pick up weekly supplies. She would get home close to nightfall, make her deliveries and then have dinner with her family. After that, she would help her mother cleaning or on a summer night, play with Daniel and the other children until it got dark.

He killed them; King Gladirus killed the children of Gerard. Some of them hadn't even managed to harness their magic, yet King Gladirus killed them in cold blood. Marta took the basin and dumped its contents over her head. The water was cold, ice cold, much like her heart. She had to be cold as ice. Gladirus showed her village no mercy; she will show him none in return. She thought, *Guardians, prepare to judge his soul because you will be receiving it very soon.*

Marta returned to the room, and took the thief's dagger from his boot. After changing into her blue dress, much like the tunic and leggings Maran's body was wearing at the Temple. She fitted the dagger into her belt and tied it tightly around her waist. Finally, she was ready.

"Daniel, Daniel! Wake up, Daniel!" Daniel awoke to Maran's desperate calling.

"Maran, what's wrong?" Daniel asked temporarily forgetting the situation they were in.

"It's Marta! She's gone!"

"What?" Daniel bolted out of bed and over to his cousin's. It was empty. He called to Andros, "Hey, wake up!"

"Huh? What?"

"Marta's gone; she probably went to the castle."

"Stupid girl, what make her...?" As the thief pulled on his boots, he noticed that his dagger was missing. "Shoot! She took my dagger. Looks like I'll have to come with you guys after all."

"But I thought you didn't want any part of this hair-brained scheme."

"She took my favorite dagger, I'm involved with this whether any of us like it or not."

"We better hurry," Maran said. "If we don't stop Marta soon, she will be as dead as me."

"Then let's go." Daniel, Maran, and the thief quietly and quickly left the room.

Daniel, Maran, and Andros hurried through the streets of the Iberian capital. Daniel mentally kicked himself for allowing Marta to go off on her own little revenge trip. He knew she was bent on vengeance for the destruction of Gerard, he should've stayed up or at least have Maran warn him if she was leaving. Well, it was too late to do anything now, all they could do now is hope they get to King Gladirus and warn him before Marta does.

"Guys, look at that." Daniel pointed to the bridge leading across the chasm. The two guards whom they met the previous day were lying on the street. Daniel checked to see if they were alive and to his relief, they were. "Marta must've been through here." The three passed them and went across the bridge. Half way across, they looked down and saw that the sewer grate was open.

"How did she get down there?" Andros asked. "I needed to use my vines to lift me out."

"Marta was always a good climber," Daniel explained. "And look, there are ledges and jagged edges for her to hang off of."

"Okay, jump," Andros commanded. "I'll use my vines to catch us."

"Wait a second," Maran said. "Since the guards are knocked out, couldn't we just go in the main entrance?" Daniel and Andros looked at each other. They didn't see any reason why they couldn't, but Marta went through the sewers. It could be a while before they would run across her and by then it may be too late for King Gladirus.

"Maran, follow the sewers and try to catch up with her," Daniel instructed. "Andros and I will go in the main entrance and warn King Gladirus." Maran nodded and flew into the sewer. Daniel continued across the bridge while Andros doubled back and picked up one of the spears that the guards were carrying. He re-joined up with Daniel and handed him the spear.

"Your magic wouldn't help us a lot in a fight," Andros commented. "Use this." Daniel took the spear which was heavy at first but magically adjusted to fit someone of Daniel's strength and size.

Daniel and Andros stepped off the bridge on the other side. Up ahead was an entrance into the cliff. Andros used a fire crystal he had to light a torch. Up ahead was a large circular cave with a large symbol painted on the floor. The symbol was the crest of the Ricardo family: a large red cross in between a quarreling serpent and dragon. In the center of the crest was a small hole.

"So, how are we supposed to get up there?" Daniel asked.

"I'll see if I can get some vines to carry us up," Andros volunteered. Daniel put the spear down on the ground. By some coincidence, the end of it fitted perfectly into the center hole. The crest began to glow. The two boys began to feel like they were being dragged upward.

Maran flew through the sewers at lightning speed. He wondered how far ahead of him Marta was. He hoped she wasn't far. This tunnel seemed to have gone forever, but it felt like he was being pulled towards something. Was it Marta wearing the crystal? He hoped it was.

Maran skidded to a stop. The tunnel suddenly curved upward. He almost didn't see it and fly right into the bedrock wall. Although it wouldn't have hurt him, he probably would have trouble finding his way back to the sewers. Maran followed the tunnel up. Occasionally, bursts of water would pass through him. Finally, he spotted the light at the end of the tunnel.

Maran appeared in a prison, most likely the same prison that Andros escaped from. It was a large stone-built room with shackles and even a torture wrack. The door was forced open and Maran had a sneaking suspicion that Marta had something to do with it. Fortunately, there were no guards in the area but Maran wasn't about to press his luck. He turned invisible and began to search for Marta.

Marta, meanwhile, was creeping through the castle wearing the dress of a servant girl. When she arrived at Ricardo Castle, she hid out while she gathered her energy for her vibro-shock then knocked out the guards using it. They didn't know what hit them. Marta climbed down the cliff and through the sewer grating. Several times she got pummeled with water (at least she hoped it was water) but she had to endure. Nothing was going to stop her from getting her revenge now. She emerged into the dungeon. She forced the door open by breaking the lock with the thief's dagger. She was inside the castle but the clothes she had been wearing since they left Icthior were dirty and wet. She had to change unless she wanted to be recognized as an intruder. She broke into the quarters of a servant and his family. Fortunately, nobody was in. Marta realized that she hadn't had a decent wash since the day before Gerard's destruction so she actually appreciated the opportunity to bathe though it was a quick one. After she was clean, she threw her old clothes out the window and donned a forest green dress belonging to the daughter of the servant, tucking Maran's soul crystal into her tunic to hide its glow and Andros's dagger to complete her picture of docile.

Now, she was trying to find King Gladirus. Since it was in the morning, he would probably be eating breakfast or maybe he was like her father and getting to work early. Thinking about her father only made her more upset. Ever since she was young, the two of them had never seen eye-to-eye, but she did love him and she knew that deep down, he loved her too. He was a well-respected member of the village despite his attitude and temper and King Gladirus killed him, for no reason at all!

Marta took several deep breaths, trying to calm her anger. She had to tread carefully. King Gladirus was almost always surrounded by soldiers or one of his Sages. And both soldiers and Sages could neutralize any form of magic, including her vibro shocks. She had to get to the throne room discreetly.

"Servant Girl," a loud voice called. Marta froze and slowly turned around. An Iberian knight, minus the helmet was staring down at her. He wasn't the one who came to Gerard the night before it was destroyed but that didn't make her hate him any less. "Go to the throne room. King Gladirus has a message that must be delivered to the guard post on the boarder with Costal Glen."

"As you command," Marta said bowing. She couldn't believe her luck. She'll have a clear shot at King Gladirus with nobody to stop her. She turned and ran off towards the throne room at the center of the palace.

Daniel and Andros materialized in a luxurious hallway. The floor was covered with plush red carpet and the walls were gold-colored. Beautiful and exotic plants were in between every other door.

"What happened to us?" Daniel asked.

"I think we were transported inside the castle," Andros guessed. "No wonder nobody could enter, you'd need a spear to be granted access."

"Come on; let's try to find Marta," Daniel said.

"Hey, hold it right there, you two!" Two knights came barreling towards them.

"Wait a minute, we're not here to fight," Daniel protested.

"Forget it, they won't listen," Andros commented as he held out his hand towards one of the plants. A single vine shot out and extended across the length of the hallway. As predicted, the knights fell over. Daniel and Andros leapt over them and dashed down the hallway.

"You know those guards are going to call in reinforcements," Daniel pointed out.

"Don't talk unless you have something important to say," Andros scolded.

"So where are we heading?"

"The throne room; if your cousin wants to kill the king, both of them will probably be there."

As predicted, King Gladirus was in his throne room with Sage Mattonda. The two were discussing the refortification of the southern boarders.

"We could have the guard post disguised as a village. That way there won't be any scrutiny from Costal Glen or Vernaclia."

"Yes, but they're bound to discover it if they try to invade from the South. There will be scrutiny anyway."

"Perhaps, how about we put one guard out in plain sight and say it's to protect the village."

"Your Highness," a guard called. "A servant girl is here for the message."

"Send her in," King Gladirus ordered. The large gold and ivory doors parted and Marta walked in, her head low and her left arm inside her right sleeve. "By the Guardians, these servants are getting so young."

"Times are changing, Your Highness," Sage Mattonda emphasized. "It's getting harder to keep up with the times." It sounded like there was a meaning to that statement but it was lost on King Gladirus. "We need you to take a message to General Rowr at the..." Suddenly the orb on Sage Mattonda's staff began to glow brightly which meant only one thing. "King Gladirus, you are in danger!"

"What?"

Marta realized that she was discovered so she had to move fast before guards could be called. She pulled out her left arm, holding Andros' dagger, from her sleeve and charged King Gladirus. With a loud war cry, she leaped up and swung the dagger at him. She was reflected as a force field appeared around the king. The Sage was generating it. Marta fell back and charged again. This time, Sage Mattonda fired an energy bolt from his staff and sent her to the ground. She lost the dagger but got up and began to do her vibro dance. King Gladirus' eyes widened. He recognized what she was about to do. He recognized it all too well.

"Marta!" Maran flew through the wall and right into her mouth, taking possession of her just as he did to Andros the previous day. Maran found it harder to possess Marta then Andros, probably because she was so strong-willed.

Daniel and Andros burst through the door with Daniel yelling, "King Gladirus, you are in danger, there's a girl here who..." he paused upon seeing Marta. "Marta, get away from him!"

"It's okay," Maran/Marta said. "I'm holding her off for now."

"That was too close for comfort," Daniel said. "Good thing you were there, Maran, looks like we're finally out of danger."

"Um... Daniel, I wouldn't exactly say that." Daniel looked around and saw that a platoon of guards was standing around them, all aiming their spears. The King must've called for guards the moment Marta began her attack.

"Uh-oh," Daniel muttered.

"Yup," Andros agreed. "Uh-oh."

Minutes later, Marta, Daniel, Andros, and Maran stood before King Gladirus and Sage Mattonda. Marta, Daniel and Andros were bound in energy chains. Maran couldn't be captured because his body was not there but the Sage threatened to kill the others if he tried anything.

"This is an outrage," Sage Mattonda said walking up and down the group. "How dare you attack our beloved King Gladirus!"

"How dare King Gladirus slaughter an innocent village!" Marta snapped back.

"Insolent child," Sage Mattonda commented as he pounded her with his staff. Marta went sprawling to the floor.

"Hey, don't you dare hit my cousin like that," Daniel barked.

"Silence, boy, or you shall suffer the same."

"Bring it on!" Marta cried struggling to stand. "You may be afraid of attacking children without leaving them helpless but I'm not afraid to attack a Sage!"

"Give it a rest," Andros said, his eyes closed indifferently. "This Sage won't listen to the ramblings of children."

Sage Mattonda walked over to him and raised his head with his staff. "Well, well, if it isn't our little pocket thief. You just escaped a couple of days ago and now you've returned? I thought you were more intelligent than that."

"It wasn't like I had much of a choice. These two..." Andros motioned with his head to Daniel and Marta. "Practically forced me here at sword point."

Sage Mattonda turned his back to them. "You three shall be executed as traitors to the crown."

"Hey, wait," Daniel protested.

"I'm not even with these clowns," Andros claimed.

"Wait a second, Sage," King Gladirus said as he stepped down from his throne. He went up to Marta and got down on one knee. To her, he asked, "Why do you want to kill me?"

"Like you don't know," Marta said acidly.

"Pretend I am stupid."

"That won't be too hard."

"King Gladirus!" Gladirus placed his arm out silencing his Sage.

"Your Highness," Daniel called. He decided to tell their story as was their original plan. Andros and Maran didn't know the whole story and Marta might tell a biased version. "About three days ago, one of your knights was sent to our village to ask one of us to bring a package for you from the neighboring village of Icthior. My cousin and I were sent to retrieve it but there was no package. During our trip, our village was attacked and destroyed. An Iberian crest was found at the remains."

"What... village?" King Gladirus asked with a little fear in his eyes.

"Gerard."

King Gladirus took a step back in surprise. He then turned to Sage Mattonda. "Sage Mattonda, explain yourself! You told me that Gerard was defecting to Morbia!"

His accusations and fierce glance didn't scare Sage Mattonda. "That was the information that I obtained, Your Highness," the Sage confirmed.

"That's a lie," Marta hissed. "If anything, Gerard is... was one of the most loyal villages in the Iberian Kingdom!"

King Gladirus turned to Marta and gazed at her with a sad look. "Young ones, though the Guardians know I probably don't deserve it, I ask for your forgiveness. We received information that some villages were ready to mutiny. I wanted to stop it before they got the chance. Alas, I was wrong." To everyone's, even the Sage's, surprise, King Gladirus dropped to both knees. "May the Guardians forgive me for what I done." Marta looked intently at the man whom she tried to kill minutes ago, her pink eyes staring into his weathered brown eyes, already filling up with tears. Suddenly, Marta gasped. The king was telling the truth, she could see it in his eyes. He was actually mourning for her village. A real murderer would never mourn for their victims.

King Gladirus turned to his Sage. "Sage, find out who distributed that information. Use any methods available to you. Heads will roll for this deception!" He turned to one of his guards. "Release them." The guard placed his spear into the energy chains and they disappeared. Marta, Daniel, and Andros stood up and stretched their bodies to get the kinks out of them.

Sage Mattonda could tell that these children were going to throw everything into chaos. However, he wasn't about ready to question the king. The only thing he could do is follow his orders. He quietly slipped out of the throne room.

Daniel, Maran, and Andros looked around at the quarters they were given. It was spacious, definitely bigger than the hotel and by far better than the dungeon. It had four single beds, all turned down for the approaching night and a dresser though it was not necessary. Light fueled by fire crystals gave the room an intimate feel. This was quarters for guest like visiting dignitaries.

"Who would've thought that I, a thief, would be staying at Ricardo Castle? And not in the dungeon either," Andros commented.

"I guess King Gladirus wanted to repay us for destroying Gerard and capturing us," Maran exposited.

Daniel, wearing the crystal found at Maran's tomb around his wrist, sat down on one of the beds closest to the door. "I had a feeling things weren't as simple as that." The other two looked at him strangely. "Part of me hoped that it was King Gladirus who wanted Gerard destroyed, it would be that easy, but now it appears that the King too was duped into this."

"Well look on the bright side, at least we get a free room." Andros spread himself out on his bed.

"Where's Marta?" Maran asked.

"She stayed behind in the throne room. King Gladirus wanted to talk to her."

Marta and King Gladirus stood facing each other in the throne room.

"Do you still want to kill me?" King Gladirus asked.

Marta lowered her head, confused and ashamed. "I don't know. You did order Gerard to be destroyed, but... I don't want to take my revenge without finding out why. Why was Gerard chosen?"

"As I said before, I had received word that the people of Gerard were going to defect to Morbia. Morbia has been our rivals since even before I was born. That's the only suspect that I can think of."

"But... why, out of all the villages in Iberia, would they pick my village?"

"I'm sorry, Young Marta, but I do not know."

Marta lowered her head. "Forgive me for my actions, Your Highness. I can understand if you want to punish me for trying to murder you."

To her surprise, King Gladirus laid a hand on her head. Her mother would often do the same thing when she did something good. But for a king to informally touch a commoner like that is all but blasphemous. It was a good thing Sage Mattonda wasn't here otherwise King Gladirus would never hear the end of it. "Marta, you are too young to be seeking vengeance. If you can learn to forgive me, then I can learn to forgive you."

Marta was surprised by King Gladirus' compassion. There was no way such a man could be responsible for the destruction of her village. To tell the truth, before Gerard was attacked, she actually respected and admired the king because of his history. He had to rise to the throne at an early age after his father passed away. His magic, whatever it was (he hardly ever uses it) was not even fully developed at the time. In short, he was in the same predicament she was in, forced to assume grownup tasks while still a child.

"Get some sleep, Marta, please."

"Yes, Your Highness."

Marta returned to the quarters she and the others were given. Climbing into her bed across from Andros's, she tried to fall asleep and was unsuccessful at first. She had too much on her mind. If King Gladirus didn't want her village destroyed, who did? Why did they want it destroyed? What role, if any, does King Gladirus play in all this? This was all very disturbing. And Marta had a feeling that it could only get worse.

Marta felt a gentle breeze blow in from the open window. The breeze had a sweet smell to it and reminded her of home. It lulled Marta into a deep sleep.

Sage Mattonda was down in the old palace archives. He had opened on his lap an ancient journal. These journals were the only physical records of the Guardians' existence. It said in legends that there were hundreds of Guardian Journals back in Tel-ána's infancy but some sort of tragedy took place and most of them were destroyed out of hatred. Now, only eleven remain, one in each kingdom. All Sages were entrusted with guarding a Guardian Journal from those who would steal it or worse, actually open it and read the forbidden scripture. Ben-Salaam, the other Iberian Sage, was actually a junior apprentice and hasn't gained enough experience to be entrusted with protecting a Guardian Journal. The Guardian Journal that Sage Mattonda was currently reading was one on ancient Tel-ána artifacts.

"Ertsi Surinam al gidara ni whok du Tel-ana. Nein recardo et eluti. Modamo Sage eluti Geddon. Nein superna ro tih de nam can olbiva. Solo acconta de Gardan ni Morbia sah et know."

As Sage Mattonda pondered over the ancient text written in the ancient language of the Guardians, a plan was forming in his mind.

Rumors had been circulating that Morbia was ready to attack the Iberian Kingdom. Perhaps those rumors are true, perhaps they weren't. And even if they weren't, they soon will be.

The next morning, Marta, Daniel, Maran, and Andros were in the dining room having breakfast with King Gladirus. Sage Mattonda came in.

"Your Highness," he addressed, "I have consulted my sources and I believe I have found the source of the faulty information. The forgers of this information were pirates, under the pay of Morbia."

"That makes sense," King Gladirus said laying his napkin on the table and getting up. "Morbia would do anything to destroy us, even turn us against ourselves."

Maran turned towards Sage Mattonda, wanting to discuss something else with him. "Sage, what about the crystal I showed you?"

"The crystal is a soul crystal. They are very hard to find, let alone operate. Someone must've wanted your soul to remain on Tel-ána and not reach the Guardian's Dimension. So they connected your soul to the crystal."

"You must've been one very popular kid," Andros commented. "I've heard that to get a soul crystal to work, an entire village must sacrifice 20 virgins and pray to the Guardians for twelve hours straight."

"I don't believe you have to do all that," Sage Mattonda commented. "But the circumstances to activate it are very rare. It was only a miracle that I was able to find any information on it at all."

"So what are you going to do about Morbia, Your Highness?" Daniel asked.

"I refuse to let something like this go without retribution. Sage Mattonda, summon Captain Garan, tell him to lead a platoon into Morbia."

Marta stood up. "I want to go too."

"I'm sorry; I can't allow that, it's too dangerous. I don't want you to get involved."

"We got involved the moment somebody came into Gerard and destroyed it. I'm going!"

"Me too," Daniel agreed also standing.

"I don't have any choice," Maran said. "Marta has my soul crystal."

"Well I'm not," Andros said. "This has nothing to do with me."

"That's a fine attitude," Daniel cracked.

"Look, it's not that I don't like you guys, but... actually, I don't like you but that's beside the point. In case you haven't been keeping track, it was you two who forced me to come here in the first place. Give me one good reason why I should go with you guys?"

"I can give you a good reason," King Gladirus said with a smile. "How about this, if you go with them and help Captain Garan protect these children, I will commute you of all charges."

"Commute my sentence?" Andros couldn't believe what he was hearing. Would he really be acquitted of all charges just for body guarding two children? There must have been a catch.

Sage Mattonda joined in, "Unless you enjoy the wrack..."

"No, no, no," Andros said quickly, not wanting to risk his good fortune. "I'll go along, I'll go along."

"Sage Mattonda, summon Captain Garan," King Gladirus repeated. The Sage nodded and the jewel on his staff glowed.

Minutes later, King Gladirus, Sage Mattonda, and the children were back in the throne room. The doors swung open and a portly-looking man with pepper-colored hair and coal dark eyes came in.

"Captain Sleuvius Garan reporting in as you ordered, Your Highness."

"Captain, I know infiltration isn't one of your strengths but we need you to journey to Morbia and investigate suspected activity against us."

HAROLD RAY

"As you command, Your Highness, I will gather a group of my best men."

"I'm afraid we'll have to keep this a secret, Captain. No guards. Instead, these four shall be your traveling companions."

Captain Garan looked at the children. He couldn't believe that these children would be coming with him instead of his highly-trained guards, but more than that, "I see only three." It was true, Maran had been invisible since before the Captain entered but he appeared right in front of the Captain. "Guardians protect me, a ghost!" He cried staggering back. Maran looked embarrassed and retreated behind Marta.

"Relax, Captain, there are no enemies here, our true enemies are in Morbia."

"Your Highness, with all due respect, I would feel much better if one of my guards accompanied me than these children."

"They're rather insistent about coming along, Captain."

"If they were to find out what we were doing, the other kingdoms would retaliate against us diplomatically," Sage Mattonda added. "This way, Morbia would not expect an Iberian Captain in the company of three children and a ghost; it is the perfect cover story."

"We can handle ourselves," Daniel assured him but the Captain was still skeptic.

"You are not even equipped properly, how will you be able to deal with whatever Morbia will throw at us."

"You are right on that one, Captain," Sage Mattonda agreed. "But I have corrected that with this." He held out a small pouch inside was sand that was white and sparkled in the natural light. "This shall give you the skills and equipment you need for what is ahead."

"Toshibi Powder? But that's only for those who have reached of age."

"Yes, unfortunately, these children were forced to come of age a lot faster than others," King Gladirus said. "Marta, Daniel, Andros, are you three ready? I should warn you, the journey ahead is very perilous. There is a chance that some of you may not come back alive."

"Let's get on with it."

"I'm ready."

"For Gerard."

Marta, Daniel, Andros, and Captain Garan stood in front of Sage Mattonda. Sage Mattonda took a handful of Toshibi Powder and blew on it. The powder magically left the Sage's hand and encircled the three children and the Captain. The powder cling itself to their clothes and began transforming them. Marta's green dress became a small gray chest plate with broad shoulder pads. Her midriff was showing and she also wore a maroon skirt and brown boots. A small red cape draped across her back. She carried a metal pole that expanded and retracted as necessary. Daniel was wearing a purple tunic and green leggings. Around his neck was a talisman like Sage Mattonda's. Andros' clothes had a blue stripe running down the sleeves and front of it. His eye patch remained on his eyes but there was a silver x on it. A dagger was holstered on each side of him. Captain Garan was in battle armor minus the helmet, the Iberian crest on his chest plate. He carried a big sword.

"Now, you are ready," King Gladirus declared. He handed the pouch of Toshibi Powder to Daniel. "Just in case." Daniel tied it to the sash that wrapped around his waist.

Marta, Daniel, Maran, Andros, and Captain Garan were sent to the cave entrance. Across the bridge were three horses. Captain Garan took one, Andros took another and Marta and Daniel shared the third.

"Just a reminder," Captain Garan said as they mounted. "I am in charge, so you must follow my instructions to the letter."

"Yeah, yeah, yeah," Andros said dismissively.

"I mean it!"

"Look, pig-face, I'm only going on this because it gets me out of the dungeon. I've got no loyalties towards you or your kingdom."

"Pig-face! Look, you miserable little…"

"Boys," Marta called. "Can we concentrate on the mission at hand?" And the horses took off.

As they left the Iberian City limits, they were unaware that someone was watching them, someone who wasn't part of Iberia.

The leader turned to one of his servants and said, "Follow them, and stop them at any cost."

A trio or horses pulled up to a small clearing in the forest. Slevius Garan, Captain of the Iberian guards dismounted and laid his hand flat on the ground. He was joined by Marta and Daniel, formerly of the town of Gerard, Maran the ghost and a thief whom went by the name Andros.

"What's wrong?" Marta asked.

"We have reached the end of our land," Captain Garan explained. "Not far is the boarder. Soon, we shall be entering Morbia territory." He said the name with almost a spit of disgust.

"I don't understand," Maran said. "What's so bad about this Morbia place?"

Andros rolled his eye. "For the love of the Guardians where have you been for the past hundred years? Trapped in a cave?"

HAROLD RAY

"Actually, it was a temple," Maran corrected rather optimistically. Andros was dumbstruck.

"Morbia and Iberia had been rivals for a long time," Captain Garan explained. "Our two countries used to be at war. We'd probably still be at war were it not for Costal Glen and Vernaclia. They made us sign a non-aggression pact."

"What's a non-aggression pact?" Maran questioned.

"We agreed that we don't like each other but promised not to attack each other," Garan exposited.

"As long as we don't attract too much attention," Daniel said. "We won't get caught."

"Like that'll happen as long as we have him with us." Andros pointed to Maran who lowered his head in shame.

"Maran, you can make yourself invisible," Marta reminded her transparent friend. "All you have to do is stick close to us and you'll be fine." That perked up Maran.

"Attack!" A voice cried out. All around them, people wearing ragged clothing appeared.

"Bandits," Captain Garan guessed. "Using invisibility armor no doubt."

"Correct, Iberian frog," said one of the bandits, an ugly paper-thin man with a hook for a hand. "The Riders of Tch'Kar to be more precise."

"Not them, not the Riders of Tch'kar!" Garan gasped. He quickly picked up Daniel and Marta and began to run away.

"What's the big deal?" Daniel asked. "They're just bandits."

"You fool," Captain Garan insulted. "The Riders of Tch'kar are not your run-of-the-mill bandits. They are a bunch of bloodthirsty cutthroats who only live for their next payment. They will resort to anything to get what they want and they don't care who the victims are, not even children!" Intelligence reports about the Riders of Tch'Kar have been in circulation among the Iberian government for about sixty years. Most of the reports consisted of reports of cattle theft and break-ins at noblemen's houses. But about six years ago, the reports started to get more graphic and more violent. Garan has never personally encountered the Riders of Tch'Kar before now.

Arrow-shape energy blasts flew by them. One of them struck one of the horses dead.

"Thief, catch!" Garan threw Marta to Andros and hauled Daniel up onto his own horse. "We must retreat into Iberian territory."

"Easier said then done," Andros commented.

"Do you want to die by their hands, you whelp?" The two remaining horses took off.

"Hey, what about Maran?" Marta asked looking around. All around them, Riders of Tch'kar on horseback, or flying, were rapidly overtaking them. "Where's Maran, I don't see him!"

"Who cares about your ghost?" Captain Garan hissed. "He's dead already so he doesn't need to worry."

"How can you be so heartless?"

"I just prefer to live."

The Riders of Tch'kar were almost upon them. Their archers were already pulling back their bows, energy arrows forming as they did so. Suddenly a pair of sinister yellow eyes appeared before them. The horses got spooked throwing their riders off. Maran appeared, his eyes glowing, his arms and head bigger than life. Maran let out an inhuman scream. The remaining Riders, those who hadn't fainted from fright, took off screaming and even crying.

"Wow, that was incredible, Maran," Daniel said excitedly.

Maran returned to his normal appearance and smiled embarrassingly at the others. "I'm sorry, I don't know what made me do that."

"Ghosts do have a habit for scaring people," Marta commented. Noticing Maran's sad look returning, she added, "When they want to, of course." That perked Maran up.

"Well, so much for stealth," Andros said. "Those Riders will obviously tell everyone they know about us."

"Perhaps not," Captain Garan replied. "People are terrified of the Riders of Tch'Kar so much they'll probably ignore their cry, but all the same, we should hurry to a village near the Morbian capital of Nutros. The Riders of Tch'Kar would not dare travel so close to the Morbian seat of power."

With one less horse, the group from Iberia quickened their pace. It was becoming nightfall very quickly and they knew they had to stop at a village soon otherwise they would be caught out in the open and vulnerable.

They soon came to the large wooden gate that separated Morbia from Iberia. The boarder was blocked off by a magic barrier. The only way through was the gate. Four guards were stationed there, two from Morbia and two from Iberia. At that moment, only the Iberian guards were visible, stationed half-way up the gate where the lookout and barracks were.

"Good evening," Daniel called out a greeting. "May we pass?"

"You want to proceed into Morbia territory?" One of the guards asked skeptically.

"We're just passing through," Marta explained.

"Very well." The Iberian guards worked the controls and the large doors parted and the magic shield was lowered. The entire process took about one minute. Once the doors were fully open, the party passed through the long narrow passage to Morbia. They looked around for the Morbian guards who monitored the gate but they were nowhere to be found, a gift from the Guardians, Captain Garan figured.

It wasn't long before they arrived at a village. The village looked much like Gerard (which made Marta and Daniel homesick). It was surrounded by a large wooden fence with a double door opening. As with most towns, a sentry stood outside.

"Good evening," Andros greeted as the group walked up. Maran was invisible and Captain Garan was wearing the cloaks of the others to cover his armor and Iberian crest. Marta could tell that Garan was annoyed about having to hide his precious Iberian symbol. "We are travelers from far away; we're just searching for a place to spend the night."

The guard looked at the group suspiciously. "What is your village?" He asked Marta. Andros opened his mouth to speak but the guard snapped, "I was not asking you, I was asking the girl."

Marta scowled at the guard and decided to respond with the truth, "I don't have a village, my village was destroyed." The guard, judging by his surprised look, wasn't prepared for that answer. He turned to Daniel.

"She and I are cousins," he said, also truthfully. "Her village is... was my village."

The guard said, "I apologize for my rudeness. We've received word of Iberian Bandits performing attacks on our villages and since then, we have been careful about whom we invite into our village."

"Iberian Bandits!" Captain Garan cried out in an incredulous tone. The guard looked at him suspiciously.

"We thought the Iberians had been dormant for years," Andros said trying to cover for Captain Garan's outburst. "It's hard to believe they would start something up now."

"We thought that too, but of course it wasn't bound to last forever. Nothing ever does, those Iberians and their savage temper and bloodlust, I knew they could never keep it in check for long."

"Could we please enter the village?" Andros asked before Captain Garan could strangle the guard right then and there.

"Of course," the guard replied and raised his spear above his head. The huge doors parted and the group was granted access inside.

"Why the nerve of that arrogant impudent..."

"Watch it, big guy," Andros warned. "It's just for the night and anyway, you shouldn't let him irritate you like that." Captain Garan was embarrassed, not just from his display at the gate, but from the fact that he was just scolded by a young thief wearing an eye patch.

The group found an Inn and settled in for the night. Captain Garan was still muttering about having to sleep in the den of the enemy. Andros took off his eye patch and rubbed the eye that the scar had swollen shut. Marta took a good look at him the scar. It almost made her sick to her stomach. For Andros, the pain that resulted from whatever made that scar must be excruciating. "Does it hurt?" She asked.

"I'm used to it."

"Have you thought about seeing a healer about that?" She asked. Andros looked at her like she just insulted him. Actually, she did. What insulted Andros wasn't the words, but the almost casual manner at which they were said.

"No," he said coldly.

"Why? It would make more sense to have a healer fix your scarred eye. Plus it wouldn't cause you so much pain."

"I keep this scar as a reminder."

"I don't understand. What do you mean by 'a reminder'?"

"A reminder of why I became a thief in the first place. A reminder of why I can trust nobody with my life." His voice was so cold, so isolated, it almost scared her.

"So what's our strategy?" Daniel asked changing the subject for fear of a fight breaking out between Andros and Marta.

"We must get in touch with the Morbian Sage, Petro Anonka," Captain Garan said. "With any luck, he will be staying at the palace."

"How do we know Sage Petro won't turn us in?" Maran asked. "I mean if the Morbians feel the same way about Iberians as Iberians do about Morbians..."

"The Sages of Tel-ána reside in a council separate from the political bodies of the kingdoms. Sage Mattonda has guaranteed us under the Sages' protection and asks us to use them to help us in our mission. Sage Petro's loyalty lies first to the Council then to the Kingdom."

"We should get some sleep," Andros said climbing into his own bed. "We'll need our wits about us as we visit the Morbian Palace." The others complied.

Just like at Ricardo Castle, Marta did not fall asleep right away. But this time, it was for a different reason. What Andros said was still ringing in her mind.

I keep this scar as a reminder, a reminder of why I became a thief in the first place. A reminder of why I can trust nobody with my life.

Marta figured that somebody must've betrayed Andros a long time ago. Or maybe it was recently, he was, after all, only a little older than she was. Whatever the length of time has passed, somebody most certainly had betrayed Andros and gave him that scar, but who and why?

The next morning, after breakfast, the group prepared to depart the village for the Morbian capital. Andros told them that assuming there are no detours, they should get there by early afternoon. Fortunately, there was a different guard then when they arrived and he didn't goad Captain Garan with talk of "the Evil Iberians."

As they traveled through the forest, a fierce wind threw them off their horses. The Riders of Tch'Kar appeared around them.

"Not these guys again," Daniel said.

"I think there's a Wind Waker with them," Marta guessed. Wind Wakers are a special breed of people. They can control elements of nature like wind, lightning, and water. They were one of the most sought-after magic groups in Tel-ána.

"Looks like we have no choice but to fight them," Andros said as the Riders of Tch'Kar surrounded them.

Daniel's talisman started to glow. A beam of energy shot out and struck one of the Riders. The blast left him on the ground, smoke billowing from his chest. The others charged. Andros placed his hands on the ground and large vines came out of the ground and grabbed several of them and snapped their necks. One of the Riders opened his mouth and a wave of invisible energy, much like Marta's vibro-shock, accompanied by an awful shriek, was launched at Captain Garan. The Captain crossed his arms in front of them and the blast could not push him back. That was his magic, he could be unmoved by physical or magical force. A number of Raiders had Marta surrounded. She couldn't use her magic without being vulnerable. Maran possessed one of the Riders surrounding Marta and made him punch one of his allies. That quickly degenerated into a slugfest between the two Riders until both fell unconscious and Maran was ejected. The others were bewildered at the fight that broke out for no reason at all so they were oblivious to Marta performing her vibro dance. She released her gathered energy in several bursts and took out the remaining Raiders.

The Riders who were fortunate enough to survive the attack were running for the hills, leaving their fallen allies. The battle was over, they had survived.

"That was actually easy," Daniel commented.

"Don't let down your guard," Captain Garan cautioned. "That was a test, to see what kind of abilities we possessed. Their next attack would be more severe. We must get to Nutros before that comes." Leaving their fallen horses, the group trekked the rest of the way to the Morbian capital.

It was late afternoon by the time the group approached the Morbian capital. Unlike Iberian Castle, the Morbian castle was centered on a large hill with a town surrounding them. A long flight of steps led up from the center of town to the castle gate.

"Look at them," Captain Garan spat. "Acting like they're Lords over all of Tel-ána. How'd I love to..."

"Okay, we understand, you don't like them," Andros snapped. "So can we get this over with?"

"Just how are we going to go through with this anyway?" Daniel asked. "I don't think they're just going to let us walk up and ask them if they destroyed Gerard."

"Our first step is to get in touch with Sage Petro," Captain Garan said. He turned to Maran. "Ghost, can you disappear and try to find him."

"I don't even know what he looks like," Maran argued.

"He's a Sage like Sage Mattonda," Marta observed. "So he might be wearing the same robes as Sage Mattonda."

"Okay, that helps. I'll go now." He grew invisible and took off.

"Come on, let's make our way towards the castle," Marta suggested. Again, Captain Garan wore the cloaks of the others to disguise himself and they journeyed into the city. The buildings were more spread out than they were in the Iberian capital. Well-off looking people walked around looking cheerful and wearing small patches of red, yellow, and green which was the colors of the Morbian King. Joyful music could be heard in the distance.

"I bet even their rats are fat," Captain Garan muttered. That earned him a scowl from Andros.

"Why is it so lively?" Daniel wondered.

"We've come during Transition Festival," Captain Garan explained. "It's when they celebrate the oncoming fall and winter. It also marks the change of command where the child would normally take over governmental duties from the father."

"You know a lot about Morbian customs," Andros commented.

"I make it a point to learn everything about my enemy," Captain Garan said seriously. "If you know your enemy, then you can beat them with ease."

"A good philosophy to have," Andros replied

Subtly, they maneuvered their way towards the base of the mountain the castle was on.

Maran floated through another wall. This room was servant quarters, much like the other ten rooms he's already checked.

"This is a big castle," he commented. "I hope I can find Sage Petro soon." He floated through another wall and into a hallway. Maran was deep in thought trying to plan his next move so he didn't hear someone walk up. What he did feel, however, was pain, intense pain. It felt like he was being sucked into something.

In fact, that's exactly what was happening. The man was holding another soul crystal. The only difference is this one confined the soul to the crystal rather than allowing it to move about in the general vicinity.

The one holding the soul crystal smiled ruefully. "And now for the others," he said.

To everyone's surprise, Maran's soul crystal stopped glowing.

"What happened?" Andros asked.

"Something must've happen to Maran," Marta said. Worried for him, she ran out of their hiding place.

"Hey wait up, Marta!" Daniel called. Andros followed. Captain Garan mumbled about children and their inability to sit still and then followed them.

They didn't need to go far. A guard appeared and grabbed Marta with one hand. Two more guards appeared and grabbed Daniel and Andros too. Captain Garan quickly drew his sword but the guards held out the children as shields. Captain Garan had no choice but to lower his weapon.

"Three children and a ghost, you certainly keep yourself in interesting company, Captain," a light-toned, aristocratic, sarcastically speaking voice said. The man who stepped from the darkness wasn't fat per se, but he was overly muscular. He was bald on top but had white hair trailing down the back of his neck. He wore armor similar to Garan's except his was endowed with the Morbian crest. "Well, my old friend, it's been a while."

"Vostock," Garan hissed.

"I am honored you remember me, Captain Garan," Vostock said with false sincerity.

"Let us go," Marta ordered. "We have a friend..."

"Do you mean... him?" Vostock held up Maran's prison crystal. The ghost gave them a pained look.

Andros was ready to slit the guard's throat when something occurred to him. How did this Vostock know Captain Garan? Was Captain Garan a Morbian spy?

Sensing Andros' confusion, Vostock said, "Your Captain and I have met on the battlefield several times in the past. His moves were always so predictable, that was why I always won."

"I don't understand; how did he know that we were here?"

"One of our junior Sages was able to detect your ghost friend. Under the right 'influence,' he revealed your plan."

"Let them go, Vostock," Garan said. "They are just children, has your heart frozen to the point where you would even torture children?"

"Garan, Garan, Garan," Vostock said shaking his head. "These are troubled times for us all. One needs to be careful where and to whom they show compassion to. There are those who might want to take advantage of it and use it as a weakness."

"So it was you who destroyed Gerard!" Marta said trying to move her arms so she could start her vibro dance.

"My dear child, this is no time to make pointless accusations. If you wish, you can bring your accusation up with King Adleton."

"Oh no," Captain Garan gasped. He remembered one time he was captured by the enemy and brought to King Adleton. The man was brutal; his torture techniques were probably the worse on Telána. If it wasn't for the non-aggression pact signed between Iberia and Morbia, then he would most likely be dead.

HAROLD RAY

Captain Garan made one last plea to Captain Vostock. "Vostock, for the love of the Guardians, let the children go. They are of no importance to you. Take me if you wish, but let them go!"

"I'm afraid I can't do that, Garan. These children were caught spying for Iberia, so they shall be charged as spies. And the punishment for spying is death!"

"The punishment for anything here is death," Captain Garan cracked.

"Don't exaggerate, Captain. Spying is considered the harshest of offenses here. However, I am not without sympathy for you and the... children. You shall be brought before King Adleton and he will decide the fitting punishment. But I doubt that it will be anything less than death."

They were taken into Morbia Castle. Once there, they were stripped of their weapons. They were then placed in anti-magic chains. The chains not only prevented them from using their magic, but immobilized their muscles so that they couldn't even move. They were then carried into the throne room.

The throne room was considerably smaller than the Iberian throne room. It was gold color although no real gold adorned the room. Captain Garan was surprised to see two thrones at the far end of the room. Last he knew, King Adleton was not married. However, one of the thrones was probably half the height of the other which suggested that somebody here was in King Adleton's favor, probably a Lord or Lady who had won over the King's favor.

"All bow before the rulers of Morbia," Captain Vostock announced although the prisoners really had no other choice. The strength from their legs have all but left.

A side door open and several aides came in. Behind them was a young girl. She had golden hair, blue eyes and a delicate face. She was dressed in a formal gown the same color as her hair. Daniel was surprised by her beauty.

"Captain Vostock, why do you call my father?"

"Forgive my rudeness, Princess Adora, but we have caught spies for Iberia."

"I see," the Princess replied neutrally and turned to one of her ladies in waiting. "Joanna, go fetch my father, he's in the library, tell him Captain Vostock requests him and that it's urgent."

"Yes, my Princess."

"Father, Princess?" Captain Garan was confused.

"That is right," Princess Adora replied before Captain Vostock could berate Garan. "I am Princess Adora Adleton, daughter to the King Randolph Adleton." Garan was surprised, he didn't know that King Adleton was now married, let alone had a daughter. Perhaps he would take it easy on them.

The doors opened and a red-haired man wearing gold armor and carrying a gold shield walked in.

"Vostock, this had better be important," the man said in a tone that betrayed irritation with the Captain. "You know well I don't like being disturbed while I'm in the library."

"Forgive me, Your Highness, but I have caught spies from Iberia."

King Adleton joined his daughter at the higher throne. "Spies, you say? Make them rise." King Adleton held out his shield and the prisoners could feel enough strength to stand and do nothing else.

"Father, they are only children!" Princess Adora said. "How can they be spies?" She stared at Daniel inquisitively. The boy could only look around the room, embarrassed at his current predicament.

"Your Highnesses, we caught them just outside the castle. They were talking about getting in touch with Sage Petro, most likely to commit some horrid act against our most noble kingdom."

"You're one to talk," Marta snapped. "You destroyed my village!"

"Silence, you little tramp!" Captain Vostock raised his hand.

"Stay your hand, Captain Vostock," King Adleton ordered. "Striking children will not improve our already diminishing reputation among the people of Morbia especially during the Transition Festival."

Captain Garan's beady eyes narrowed. King Adleton was falling out of favor with the Morbian people? If this was true, then he couldn't have destroyed the Iberian village. Doing so would risk a new war with Iberia and further tarnishing King Adleton's reputation as the reformed war monger. And if there was anything definite that Captain Garan learned about King Adleton, it's that he values his reputation almost as much as he values his life.

"Child, I don't know who told you this lie, but I assure you I did not ask your village to be destroyed."

"What?" Daniel gasped. "But Sage Mattonda told us that whoever destroyed the village is here in Morbia!"

"If someone from Morbia did destroy your village, which I highly doubt, it was not authorized by me."

"Gee, where have I heard that before?" Andros asked sarcastically. He was booted in the stomach by Captain Vostock.

"Vostock!" Princess Adora snapped.

"Forgive me, Your Highness," Captain Vostock said. "But I did not want him to disrespect you."

King Adleton turned towards Captain Garan and the children. "What proof do you have that it was Morbia who initialized this attack on your village?"

"Well..." Marta didn't want to tell him that the only proof they have was Sage Mattonda's tip.

"That's what I thought," King Adleton said as he stood. "Throwing around weak accusations without proof, I thought you Iberians were more intelligent then that."

"Wait a minute," Marta said. "Ask Sage Petro, he will..."

"Sage Petro does not have authority over me," King Adleton interrupted her. "And without any evidence to back up your claim, I have no choice but to consider you spies on a mission to disrupt the sanctity of our kingdom." He got up and aimed his hand. Energy began forming in his hand.

"For the love of the Guardians, they are only children!" Captain Garan cried. "How do you think your people will react when they discover that you used your magic to harm children?"

"These children were caught spying for Iberia. I have no choice but to make them an example to others who might think about betraying me." Captain Vostock smirked at them.

"Captain Garan, can't you block the blast?" Andros asked.

"Not while these inhibitors are on us."

"Good-bye," King Adleton said like he didn't enjoy this. "May the Guardians accept you." A golden energy blast launched out towards the Iberians.

Captain Garan tried to muster up strength to at least take the blunt of the energy blast launched by King Adleton, but no matter how hard he tried, he couldn't. The magic-suppressing bonds placed on him and the others prevented them from even moving, let alone using their magic. Even after all this time, he still couldn't believe how heartless King Adleton was, killing an enemy soldier was one thing, but to willingly cause the deaths of three children, that was too inhuman; and in front of his own daughter, no less. Well, there was nothing Garan could do about it now. He closed his eyes and braced for the end.

An invisible wall formed between the prisoners and their doom. The energy was dispersed into nothingness. Sage Mattonda walked in along with a dark skinned man wearing the same type of clothes.

From the strange flower crest on his belt buckle, Garan concluded that this was Sage Petro, the Morbian Sage.

"What's the meaning of this?" King Adleton asked.

"King Adleton, these children are under the protection of the Council of Sages," Sage Mattonda announced holding up a scroll. The Sage's seal could clearly be seen binding the rolled-up piece of parchment. "I have guaranteed that the council would protect them while they undertake a mission of utmost importance. Any manner of attack against the children is considered an act of defiance against the Council of Sages. Do you dare challenge us, King Adleton?"

"You have no authority here, Sage," King Adleton replied. "Only my rule matters."

"Not according to the people." Sage Petro gestured with his own staff to an outside window. He and King Adleton looked out to see a large crowd gathering at the foot of the castle, the guards using any means necessary short of murder to keep them from storming the palace.

"If you wish to defy the Council of Sages, that is one thing," Sage Mattonda commented coming up behind them. "But to defy your own people is an action not even a Sage would undertake. Further more; killing an Iberian official is considered a breach of the Treaty of Harland. You are treading very dangerous waters, Your Highness."

"Father, release them," King Adleton's daughter, Princess Adora, pleaded. "I have no desire to make an enemy of the Council of Sages or the Iberians and no King would defy his own people. They would exile you to Darinka." The kids couldn't believe their good fortune, not only was Sage Mattonda vouching for them on behalf of the Council of Sages, but now the King's own daughter was sticking up for them, even if it was for the safety of her father. Captain Vostock looked like he was just slapped in the face.

King Adleton sighed and touched his daughter's cheek affectionately, "You know I can never say no to you, my daughter.

Guards, release them." The bonds were removed and the group spent a minute getting their strength back. Maran was freed from his prison. The soul crystal around Marta's neck started to glow again. The ghost returned to his friend's side relieved.

"Your Highness, these children were not spying on you," Sage Petro said. "They were trying to find out who was responsible for an attack on an Iberian village. It is possible that the culprits are hiding here in our very own kingdom."

"Impossible," King Adleton spat. "I would never allow such a thing."

"Your Highness," Sage Mattonda addressed. "I understand your feelings, but we must find these culprits and bring them to justice. The next village they destroy might be one of your own if you don't mind me saying so."

King Adleton let out another sigh. "Your words are wise, Sage, something I did not expect from an Iberian." Captain Vostock saw that Captain Garan was barely holding back an impulse.

"Father," Princess Adora called. "Why don't you have them visit Harold in Kashuto? If the Sage is correct in the fact that the culprits are bandits, he will know every action taken by the underground." Like all societies, Tel-ána had a dark side, improper use of magic, mistreatment of people from their own kingdoms and other such atrocities.

"A good idea, my dear Adora," King Adleton agreed. He turned to the Iberians. "On the north coast of Kashuto there lives a man who has often performed operations for me in the Tel-ána Necromon. Go to see him and he shall be able to give you the answers you seek." Princess Adora snuck out of the throne room while King Adleton was instructing the Iberian party.

"We thank you for your understanding, patience, and council, Your Highness," Sage Mattonda said as he led Marta, Daniel, Andros, Maran, and Captain Garan out of the throne room.

"Sage Mattonda," Marta said once they were alone. "You told us that Morbia was behind the attacks on Gerard."

"Yes, I did and that was what I was told. This is very disturbing; someone is playing all of us for fools. But if this man is as informative as King Adleton claim, then we shall find out the truth soon enough. Now go to the Shadowdancer Inn and wait for me. We shall take off at nightfall."

"But what about bandits or the Riders of Tch'Kar?" Captain Garan asked. "The Riders have already attacked us twice."

"I shall come with you on this trip. They wouldn't dare attack a Sage, and even if they were crazy enough to do so, it would be pointless."

"What will you do while we're at the Inn?" Daniel said.

"I need to get some information from Sage Petro. Don't worry; I shall be with you soon." The Iberian party went down to the drawbridge and discovered that the crowd, had there ever been one at all, had long since dispersed.

As soon as they had left the castle, Sage Mattonda gripped his staff in both hands and touched the tip of it to the ground. Sage Mattonda's body faded into the wall and became dark, like a shadow. He moved through the halls of the castle like a phantom. He descended into the palace archives, which also served as Sage Petro's quarters. He revealed himself and began looking through the piles of books and parchments for what he was looking for. He finally found it, the Guardian Journal that all Morbian Sages have been guarding ever since the beginning. Sages weren't even allowed to open their own Guardian Journals let alone the Journals under the guardianship of other Sages. What Sage Mattonda was doing was illegal by all religious and legal laws, but if what Sage Mattonda suspected was true, then the laws were about to change.

But first, he needed to make a copy of the Guardian Journal so he could study it more effectively without arousing the suspicions of Sage Petro. It would be difficult, duplicating objects was not a

HAROLD RAY

natural form of magic, but nevertheless, it was not impossible for a Sage to perform such an act. Sage Mattonda placed one hand on the journal and the other hand on the table.

"Parkos nea dupla!" Sage Mattonda cried. However, his magic bounced off a force-field and a blast of energy emitting from the book itself sent him crashing into a pile of books. There was some sort of barrier that kept any magic from touching it. That meant that he would have to find another way to find the information he sought.

Sage Mattonda heard footsteps and the sound of a door opening. He quickly placed the Guardian Journal back on the shelf it was kept on. He became a shadow just as Sage Petro opened the door. He leaned his staff against the wall and sat down at the desk. He looked at the pile of books that Sage Mattonda accidentally knocked over.

"I must start cleaning things up here," he said. Sage Mattonda quietly chanted another spell and phased right through the wall and out of the castle.

Princess Adora sat in front of her vanity. She was still thinking about the Iberians. They freely stood up to her father, an action that would cause death for a Morbian (or anyone else for that matter). It was the luck of the Guardians that he accepted her recommendation to have them go see Harold. Most of the time, he doesn't even listen to her suggestions. And during those few times that he did, found some sort of fault in her plan.

Adora got up and went to her window. The sun was setting in the horizon. It was a scene that she has viewed so many times before that she could see it even in her sleep. For most of her life, she never had been outside the town. Whenever her father would receive foreign dignitaries, she would sit in a balcony overlooking the throne room and soak in the visitor's personality, whether it was benign or malevolent. She often imagined visiting the dignitary's kingdom and see if all the people were like the dignitary.

That was what she wanted to do, she wanted to get out of the castle and see all the kingdoms of Tel-ána, meet as many people as she could. She wanted to be as experienced as the foreign dignitaries were. Perhaps this was her chance.

She turned to her servant, "Joanna, please bring me ink and paper... and a new quill too."

"As you command," the small woman said bowing. As soon as she left the room, Adora went into her chest and pulled out an old brown cloak, one that her father had worn in his nomad days before the previous Morbian King, Orcus, groomed him to become a representative to the king and eventually to the title of king upon King Orcus's death.

"I must say, I am surprised," Captain Garan admitted as the party sat in the lounge area of the Shadowdancer Inn.

"Surprised about what?" Andros asked.

"The King's daughter."

"What do you mean?"

"King Adleton and I have crossed paths once before," Captain Garan explained. "In that encounter, he gave the impression of a dictator who would tolerate no form of insubordination, a man incapable of tolerance let alone love. And now he has a daughter, I don't see how that is possible."

"It's because of Lady Miya," the jovial proprietor of the inn said walking by.

"Who's Lady Miya?" Marta asked.

The innkeeper chuckled, "'Who's Lady Miya?' What kingdom are you from?"

Everyone paused, afraid of mentioning Iberia for fear of a mob scene starting. "Estrellia," Andros replied as Captain Garan turned to keep the innkeeper from finding out their true point of origin.

"Oh, Estrellia, a great country, I guess its okay to tell you."

The innkeeper explained that Lady Miya was a noblewoman who grew up not far from the home village of King Adleton. Adleton, who simply went by his first name Randolph back then, was smitten with her and she was with him though neither of them knew that at the time. When the war between their two nations was starting to heat up, Lady Miya, an Iberian spy, convinced Randolph to aid the other side giving Iberian forces the advantage they needed to take the village. When the villagers discovered what had happened, they branded Randolph a traitor and sent him away. For over twenty years, Randolph wandered Tel-ána learning how to fight and how to survive.

But back at home, things weren't going too well for Lady Miya. The village was under the control of a despicable Iberian dictator, mean and cruel even from the perspective of the Iberian immigrants who integrated themselves with the villagers soon after Randolph was exiled. The Iberian government still recognized it as a Morbian village and refused to send aid making the dictator precisely that in every meaning of the word. Miya herself, after losing her fortune and noblewoman status to the very same Iberians she helped, was forced to become a Comfort Woman, performing various services for the people of the village just to get enough money for food. It was ironic a noblewoman betrayed her country but only ended losing everything but the clothes on her back.

When he received word of the goings on in the village, Randolph felt honor-bound to liberate his village even though they had branded him a traitor two decades before. He pleaded with the Morbian King Orcus for assistance. Orcus was only too happy to lend three squadrons as an advance force while he stood off in the distance with the army ready to intervene should the need arise. As it turned out, the need never arose because Randolph along with the squadrons Orcus gave him was enough to decimate the bulk of the garrison there and sent the remaining forces fleeing for the hills. The village was free and Randolph was made part of the king's personal entourage and since King Orcus had no heir of his own, Randolph was given the name Adleton, which meant redeemer in the ancient language that was used by the Guardians and was made King of Morbia upon King Orcus's death.

As for Lady Miya, though he had the chance to kill her, King Adleton did not. He loved her too much to kill her in revenge. Instead he made her a servant and had her work off her redemption. By the time the debt was paid, Miya realized how much she really did care for Adleton.

"The rest they say is history," the Innkeeper finished. "It's Morbia's greatest love story, sung at all the festivals and each year throughout King Adleton's reign."

"Morbian propaganda," Captain Garan mumbled under his breath.

Unfortunately, the Innkeeper heard something from the Captain's mouth and turned towards him with a scowl. "What did you say?"

"Don't worry about him, he's always grumpy," Andros dismissed. "The people must really cherish him."

"Some do, some don't," the Innkeeper said. "Lady Miya died in childbirth. The Princess Adora is their only child."

Then it's no wonder King Adleton agreed to Adora's request so easily, Marta thought.

It was then that Sage Mattonda came up to them. "It is time to leave," he announced.

The Innkeeper noticed the small symbol embedded in Mattonda's talisman. "You're an Iberian?" He gasped taking a step back as if afraid of being stung.

"I am under business here from the Council of Sages, not the Iberian government," Sage Mattonda said calmly. "If you like, I can show you my authorization papers."

The Innkeeper relaxed. "No, that's all right. We have never forgiven the Iberians for what they did to His Highness and the good Lady Miya. That is why people here hold such contempt for the Iberians."

"Well, the last thing I want to do is bring trouble on your Inn," Sage Mattonda said. "In any case, my companions and I will take our leave now."

The Innkeeper nodded, "Guardians be with you, Noble Sage."

"And you, Noble Innkeeper."

The sun was almost setting as the Iberian party got ready to leave. "We'll only be going as far as the Morbian boarder," Sage Mattonda explained. We shall rest there."

"Have you found any information regarding this Harold person?" Captain Garan asked.

"When we arrive at a town, I'll send a message to the other Sages requesting for information regarding Harold."

As Daniel lifted a saddlebag onto his horse, he accidentally knocked a sleeping mat down causing it to yelp in pain. Immediately, everybody took out their weapons and aimed it at the mat.

"A shape changer," Sage Mattonda identified as he waved his staff over the mat. The mat turned into Princess Adora who had changed from her golden dress to a simple brown tunic and cloak. "Princess Adora, what are you doing here?"

"Forgive me," she pleaded in a voice entirely different from the strong almost uppity voice they were listening to in the throne room. "But I didn't want anybody to see me leave the palace."

"When your father finds out you're gone, he'll probably send the entire Morbian army after us," Captain Garan snapped.

"I left my father a letter. I have never been outside the city let alone the kingdom. Please don't take me back."

"Why are you doing this anyway?" Daniel asked.

"Like I said, I have never been outside the kingdom. I think my father doesn't want me to be influenced by the outside world. He keeps me inside the castle but that even makes me want to see the world a whole lot more. Please take me along, I promise I won't be a burden."

Sage Mattonda sighed, "very well, but if we run into your father or anyone who's looking for you, you're letting them take you home, all right?"

"Yes, I agree."

"Well, let's go, Princess," Andros said rolling his eye at the thought that he was going to be responsible for guarding another child.

"Don't call me Princess," Adora requested. "I don't want people to recognize me as the Princess, it might make them uncomfortable. Call me Ada."

"Why do you want us to call you Ada?" Marta asked.

"It's my initials. Adora Desiree Adleton. Ada."

"Daniel, give her the Toshibi Powder," Sage Mattonda instructed. "Even dressed like that, she is going to stick out."

"Of course, my Sage," Daniel responded. Princess Adora threw off the cloak to reveal a blue smock and leggings as Daniel took a handful of Toshibi Powder and threw it. It stuck onto her clothing and transformed it into a silver tunic with flared sleeves, silver skirt and leggings. A large Y-shaped blade was attached to a crossbow mounted on her forearm. The group mounted up again.

"May I ride with you, young Iberian?" Ada asked.

"If that is your command, Your Highness," Daniel said blushing.

"That is not my command that is my request. Will you let me?"

"Daniel, your face is turning colors, are you all right?" Maran asked.

"I'm fine," Daniel hissed to the ghost who immediately retreated over by Marta. "I'd be honored if you would ride with me."

"Thank you, young Iberian."

"You can call me Daniel... if you wish."

Ada chuckled. "Daniel, all right, Daniel." They rode beyond the boarders of the Morbian Capitol and into the forest.

Meanwhile, they were being spied on by two of the Riders of Tch'Kar.

"Which one is it?" One asked.

"She's on the back of the horse with the medallion boy."

"I see. Can we attack now?"

"You know they have a Sage with them."

"I don't care if they have a Guardian with them, I want some action!"

"Down, boy, you'll get your chance."

The group had been traveling for a few hours. They stopped and Sage Mattonda and Captain Garan checked the map Sage Petro gave them.

"If we travel the boarder between Morbia and Estrellia, we should reach Kashuto by tomorrow night," Captain Garan said. Rolling up the map, he added, "That should reduce our travel time rather than traveling through Costal Glen.

"Yes, but we must take it easy because we'll be traveling through the Riders of Tch'Kar territory. We'll give ourselves three days leeway."

"But my Sage, if the crisis is as dire as His Highness King Gladirus says then we must get to Harold as quickly as possible."

Suddenly the orb on Sage Mattonda's staff started to glow. Andros pointed that out.

"We're about to be attacked!" Sage Mattonda cried just before the Riders of Tch'Kar bounded out of their hiding places and attacked. The Iberians and Princess Adora backed themselves into a circle.

Sage Mattonda held out his staff. A wave of energy threw a column of Riders back allowing the group to gallop through. Daniel joined in plowing the way through using his talisman. Maran possessed one of the Riders and used his wind magic to further clear the way. But it wasn't long before others began storming them. Captain Garan drew his sword and struck them down.

"Get them off their horses," one cried. Their horses were pummeled with energy bolts. Daniel was pinned underneath his dead horse.

"Marta, help me!" He called out.

"Daniel!" Marta started her dance to gather energy for a vibro-shock blast but a staff knocked her down, dazing her. As the Rider was about to go in for the kill, Andros drew his dagger and threw it. The dagger landed in the Rider's neck killing him.

A large dragon rose out of nowhere and started thrashing the Riders. The Riders quickly withdrew. The dragon turned and lifted the dead horse from Daniel. After setting it aside, it began to shrink and transformed back into Ada.

"Thanks, Ada," Daniel said smiling weakly. Ada blushed. Then she screamed as an invisible force lifted her off the ground and began dragging her away. "Ada, no!"

"Help me!" She cried.

"Mighty Sage, please use your magic!" Captain Garan pleaded.

"I shall do my best!" Sage Mattonda responded. The purple orb on his staff began to glow. Ada felt herself being pulled in two separate directions. It was straining her body. "It's no use," Sage Mattonda cried. "Even with my magic, the force is too strong." Sage Mattonda released his magical grip on Ada allowing the Princess to be carted away.

"Whoever kidnapped her must have the same powers as your father, Marta," Daniel observed. Marta winced. Even though she knew that it wasn't King Gladirus who ordered the massacre of her village, it still hurt Marta to hear others talk about her father.

"We have to go after her," Captain Garan said.

"Why should we?" Andros asked.

"Ada said she left her father a note," Maran commented. "If he finds us without her, he'll probably kill us... I mean kill you guys."

"Oh, good point." Everyone took off after Ada's floating body. Ada was trying to use her transformation magic to take the form of heavy animals and objects but the instigator of the magic was obviously experienced enough to keep his focus despite the rapid shift in body mass and personal weight.

"Maran, go inside her!" Sage Mattonda instructed. Maran tried but no matter how fast he flew, he couldn't catch up with her.

Daniel was the fastest of the living bunch, he was almost able to reach out and grab her when an invisible force slammed into him and pinned him to the ground. Marta, Sage Mattonda, Captain Garan and Andros followed suite. A person stepped from the shadows, a man with a full beard and matted black hair. More people stepped from the shadows. One of them formed nets made out of light and threw them over the Iberians.

"Who are you?" Sage Mattonda asked. "How dare you attack a Sage!"

"Be silent!" The bearded man hissed. Then he turned to his friends. "Bring him to Chief Anánzu."

"Who's Anánzu?" Andros asked. Nobody gave him an answer.

"Be silent," the bearded man said again. "Prisoners are not to speak."

Their weapons were taken away from them and they were bonded in magic-suppressing energy chains.

"Seems like I've been captured more times in the past three days than the past three weeks combined," Andros muttered. "Must be the company I'm in."

"Just who are you anyway?" Marta asked their captors after kicking Andros in the shins.

"We are the Riders of Tch'Kar."

"At least we'll be with Ada," Maran said.

The bearded man stared at the ghost. "Ada?"

"Yeah, she's the girl that you just kidnapped," Daniel reminded them.

"We have no prisoner by that name. You are the only ones we have captured today." Everybody revealed a confused look.

The Iberians were herded into a camp. Wooden sticks held up cloth walls and roofs. People of all types were sitting around, and most of them were actually having a good time. A large canopy was set up in the center. A map of Tel-ána was spread out on a center table.

"Chief Anánzu, we have captured these during our mission," the bearded man explained. Everyone gasped with surprise.

Chief Anánzu was a woman. Her hair was an unnatural purple color. It was short, but the bangs on her right side were long and extended over one of her eyes. Her visible eye was the same color as her hair. She was dressed in a kimono and long silk skirt. She was actually good looking despite her unusual appearance.

"Anánzu's a woman!" Andros realized.

"Who are you people?" Sage Mattonda asked.

"My name is Anánzu, leader of the Riders of Tch'Kar."

"Where is Ada?" Daniel asked forcefully.

"We did not kidnap your friend."

"But she was kidnapped by the Riders of Tch'Kar. And you just said you were leader," Marta pointed out.

"The group that kidnapped your friend is outlaws. We are the real Riders of Tch'Kar!"

King Adleton crumpled up the letter with one hand and threw it on top of the brown cloak found by Vostock. "How could she," he asked. "Have I done something wrong?"

"I assure you, Your Highness, it is not your fault. I am sure those Iberian whelps kidnapped her and planted the note," Captain Vostock said.

"No, Captain, as embarrassing as it is to admit this, it is my fault, at least partly. I kept her sheltered for so long that the temptation was just too great." As much as Adleton hated to admit it, it was his fault. When his now deceased wife Miya asked him literally on her deathbed to protect their daughter at any cost, he believed it meant shielding her from all the dangers of the outside world. He believed that if she did not know what the outside world had to offer, she wouldn't abandon her family and thus be safe. Unfortunately, that idea came back to haunt him ten-fold. The Iberians simply provided her with the opportunity. King Adleton turned to Vostock and said, "Captain Vostock, please find my daughter. Bring her back safely."

Captain Vostock bowed before his king. "And what do you want me to do with the ones who kidnapped her?"

"I do not care what happens to them; just bring back my daughter safe and sound." This was the truth. As much as Adleton hated the Iberians, he'd rather have his daughter back than anything else.

"Your wish is my command, my King." As Vostock turned to leave, he smiled. He will love taking out that obese Iberian lapdog, Garan. He shall pay for the dishonor he brought to Morbia and to himself.

Captain Vostock arrived in the guard barracks. He gathered up twenty of his knights, the ones that he knew would follow him to the ends of Tel-ána and beyond. He knew they were heading for Kashuto, so if he went there as well, then he will surely come upon them. Kashuto was the second-smallest kingdom in Tel-ána (the first being the island kingdom of Costal Glen), and he knew where Harold lived so it that will make this mission all the more easy.

"What do you mean the real Riders of Tch'Kar?" Sage Mattonda asked the woman called Anánzu. "There is only one Riders of Tch'Kar, and those are the ones that kidnapped Prin… I mean Ada."

"For a Sage, you really don't know much," Anánzu commented. "First of all, we know that the girl you call Ada is really Princess Adora of the kingdom of Morbia. We have informants in Morbia as well as other kingdoms." Nobody denied it. "And as to answer your question, Sage, we are the true Riders of Tch'Kar."

"But if you are the true Riders of Tch'Kar, then who have been attacking us since we left Iberia?" Maran asked.

"Those are terrorists, bandits who have been tainting our name for their own selfish greed." Anánzu went on to explain that the Riders of Tch'Kar were originally formed seventy years ago by her father. When he died, as his only child, she inherited the leadership mantle. The others didn't care that she was a woman, she was the child of their leader and that was good enough for them. The original purpose of the Riders of Tch'Kar was to unite the twelve kingdoms of Tel-ána into one government. They did that by performing small raids on villages in various kingdoms, hoping it would cause the kingdoms to unite against them. However, they were betrayed from within and since then, bandits have been performing atrocities such as murders, group rapes and even destroyed entire villages, all in the name of the Riders of Tch'Kar. Eventually, the reputation of the Riders of Tch'Kar became notorious.

"So what do you want with us?" Daniel asked.

"We want to put a stop to these evil Riders. You want to rescue Princess Adora. I propose that we join forces."

"Join forces?" Captain Garan parroted.

"That is correct, join forces. I'll let you talk amongst yourselves. When you made a decision, tell the guards." And with those words, she left them.

"I do not trust her," Sage Mattonda said.

"But what choice do we have?" Captain Garan countered. "I saw the map. They know where these evil Riders are, and they might have Princess Adora. I believe we should join forces."

"I agree with the Sage," Andros said. "These guys aren't to be trusted."

"You wouldn't trust your own father," Marta said scowling. Andros' eyebrow twitched at that comment. "We have to trust them."

"You're too trusting, Marta," Andros countered. "Eventually, that's going to be your downfall."

"I don't trust everybody," Marta argued. "But I have a feeling Anánzu and these Riders of Tch'Kar can be trusted."

"All right, that's enough," Sage Mattonda scolded. "Marta and Captain Garan are right. Trustworthy or not, we need them to lead us to where Ada is being captive. We'll have to trust them... for now, anyway."

However, distrust was being expressed on both sides. Anánzu was meeting with her advisors.

"Chieftain, they can not be trusted," one argued.

"There have a knight and a Sage with them," another added. "They obviously work for the Iberian government; I concur that they can not be trusted."

"I understand your concern, but the evil Riders are growing stronger with each passing month. More and more are joining their cause and our opportunity for redemption is slowly slipping away. We need to become more powerful and the Iberians can help us do that."

"Are you sure this is simply about the evil Riders?" A third advisor asked.

"What do you mean?"

"You do know who's in charge of the evil Riders, don't you? Anánzu, we must be cautious, not reckless."

"So noted, but despite what you may think, my sole thought is of redeeming our name."

A soldier came in. "Forgive me for intruding, Chief Anánzu, but the Iberians have reached a decision."

"And...?"

"They have agreed to your terms."

"Excellent. Release them and bring them to me, we need to do some things before our final strike." They nodded and left.

"Anánzu," Jeffrey (the advisor who asked her if this was about the evil Riders) called. "Why are we investing so much effort in these Iberians? Or is it the girl?"

"So you noticed too."

"Anánzu, you must put it in the past. Raising the dead is something only the Guardians can do. And re-opening old wounds is something only the suicidal are willing to do."

"What makes you think I'm re-opening it?" Anánzu asked looking away. Her voice was solemn. "Maybe it hasn't healed from being broken the first time." Jeffrey sighed and left. Anánzu sighed and recalled the pink-eyed girl who was with the Iberians. "The resemblance is uncanny," she muttered before leaving.

Ada looked around at her surroundings. She was in a room made from stone and clay. A large shelf (she assumed it was a bed since it was long enough to fit someone of a human size) ran along a whole wall. There was nothing else inside, nothing that she could use to escape. Not that she could escape even if given the chance. After she was captured, the Riders beat her around until she was on the verge of falling unconscious. They then summoned a healer for her just so they could beat her up again. It was like a torture. After doing what they wanted with her, they then put her into magic suppressing chains and placed her in a cell.

In front of her stood their leader (she could tell that by the obnoxiously smug face he was showing). "Don't bother trying to break free Princess," the leader Zachariah said in a high-pitch, almost psychotic voice. Ada tried to hide her shock at him finding out who she really was. "Oh yes, we know you're really Princess Adora Adleton, daughter of King Randolph Adleton of the Morbian kingdom."

Ada tried not to let her fear of her exposure show. "So what do you plan to do with me? If it's money that you want, my father will..."

"Oh we're not interested in anything you can provide, Princess," Zachariah said chuckling as he lifted her chin and, in turn, her head up to face his yellow-green eyes. "It's what our boss wants."

"Who's your boss?"

"Oh please, like I would tell you. I'll let you get some sleep now. You're going to need it, because tomorrow the real fun begins," Zachariah said as he left. Ada summoned up her last ounce of strength and tried to break the chains but it was no use, she was too weak from the torture she received from the Riders of Tch'Kar. The only thing she could do was limp over to her bed and cry herself to sleep, silently begging someone, anyone, to come and rescue her.

"I thank you for agreeing to join forces with us," Anánzu said to the Iberians when they were escorted into her tent. "However, before we set out on our mission, we must take care of some things first."

"I knew there had to be a catch," Andros said crossing his arms.

"What seems to be the problem?" Sage Mattonda asked business-like.

"A few days ago, many of our forces were captured. They're being held in a separate location from Ada. If we're to have any chance of rescuing Ada; we'll need all the troops we can muster, so we must rescue them before we set out. Will you please help us?"

"Why should you even ask?" Sage Mattonda asked. "Of course we will."

"Thank you, I just thought I should ask for my own peace of mind. Here is what we're going to do. Our best bet is to sneak them out one at a time. You two..." she pointed to Marta and Daniel. "Shall cover the escape route while they..." she moved her finger until it faced Andros and Captain Garan. "And I will sneak them out. Ghost, I want you to distract the evil Riders. I want the Sage to stay behind with reinforcement forces just in case."

"That is going to take a while," Sage Mattonda noted.

"I know but it's the only way we can do it without alerting the evil Riders. We set off tomorrow at daybreak."

When daybreak approached, Marta, Daniel, Andros, and Captain Garan along with Anánzu and a small party of her Riders of Tch'Kar set off. The evil Riders had set up camp along the bottom of a cliff. A wooden fence surrounded dozens of men and women and even some children. There were large wooden spikes all along both sides of the fence including the door.

Maran flew throughout the camp screaming at the top of his voice. Immediately the evil Riders were sent for the hills. Meanwhile, Marta, Daniel, Andros, Captain Garan, and Anánzu quietly went up behind the spiked fence.

"I'm not sure even I can pick that lock without getting pricked," Andros complained.

Anánzu turned to Marta. "Marta is your name, right?" Marta nodded. "Well Marta, I noticed you have a quarterstaff with you. You can use it to knock down the spikes."

"But I don't know how," Marta said.

"All right, then let me do it." Marta handed her the metal staff she was given when King Gladirus gave her the Toshibi Powder. Anánzu started twirling it with expert precision. Soon, the staff was a spinning blade, knocking off spikes from the door. Soon, the door was clear enough for Andros to safely move in and pick the lock.

"Everybody has to get out now quickly," Anánzu instructed. They hurried out, each offering thanks to their saviors.

"The prisoners are escaping!" Someone cried out.

"Marta, hurry and intercept them," Anánzu instructed.

"Okay. Come on, Daniel."

"Right." The two former residents of Gerard hurried to stop the evil Riders before they could re-capture their prisoners. Daniel used his talisman to fire a burst of energy that knocked several of them down. Marta knew she didn't have enough time to do a full vibro-dance so she just moved her arms and sent out several quick bursts of vibration energy at them. Fortunately it was enough to halt them from advancing, at least temporarily.

"Hurry, you two, we're leaving," Andros called out. Marta and Daniel hurried to leave but the two evil Riders who were targets of Marta's small vibro-shocks grabbed them.

"No!" Anánzu cried as she threw Marta's staff like a javelin. It stabbed right through the evil Rider's arm. Marta kicked him, withdrew her staff and broke free. Putting the staff away, Marta quickly gathered her vibration energy and released it. Since the blast was almost at point blank range, the evil Rider holding Daniel lost his head literally. Marta and Daniel retreated towards the others.

"Thank you, Miss Anánzu," Marta said.

"You are welcome, meina utar, now come on let's go."

Marta wondered what Anánzu called her.

They returned to Anánzu's base camp where there were joyous reunions all around. Apparently, those captives were from Anánzu's home village, which have been constantly under attack by the evil Riders. One night, the evil Riders snuck in and kidnapped them all. There was no struggle. The evil Riders were going to hold them for ransom until Anánzu's Riders of Tch'Kar and the Iberians were able to free all of them. "Thank you all," Anánzu said to the Iberians once they all returned to their base camp. "You not only helped us gain an edge over our enemies, but you proved your honor and worthiness. Please, rest while we prepare our plan for tonight."

Zachariah spoke with his chief advisers. "If what we were told was accurate, then they will come and rescue her."

"You are aware that there is a Sage with them," Advisor Leroy said. "If he uses his magic, we won't stand a chance."

"Don't worry about the Sage. In the mean time, we shall prepare for their arrival. We'll kill them all."

"Are you insane?" Advisor Henry asked. "The boss will..."

"The boss can survive by himself. We must remember the plan. We must stop the Iberians at all cost."

"If they do plan on attempting a rescue mission, they will most likely attack at nightfall. Tonight is a dark night, with no moon. Perfect cover for a rescue party," Leroy said. Zachariah agreed with him.

"We will set our troops here, here, and here in a snare maneuver. We'll trap them inside the inner keep. Since none of them can fly, it will be easy picking them off."

In her prison, Ada tried her hardest to get some sleep. There had been no end to the torture she endured at Zachariah's hands. At times, it felt like someone was draining the very magic from her. She never felt more vulnerable in her life.

"Father… anybody… please help me!"

Marta tried shifting her metal staff to the other hand like Anánzu did earlier but only succeeded in knocking herself on the head again. She grunted as a slight shift of the thumb caused the staff to retract to a reduced length. When King Gladirus bestowed on her the Toshibi Powder, it gave her a weapon that, according to Sage Mattonda, fitted their inner soul. But Marta couldn't see how a metal pole that could extend to various lengths be a reflection of her inner soul. She scowled at it, like it was the cause of Gerard's destruction.

"The secrets of the universe aren't normally stored in an object," Anánzu commented as she walked up to Marta.

"I… I just want to make myself stronger," Marta said even though she didn't know why she was trying to explain herself to the leader of the 'true' Riders of Tch'Kar. "If I could only be stronger, maybe I can prevent another attack like the one on my village."

"You are a lot stronger than you think you are; all you need is the knowledge." Anánzu took a wooden staff from one of her soldiers who was passing by with a stack of them and twirled it with supreme professionalism. "Go ahead; try to strike me with your staff." Marta let out a whine. "Come on, just do it." Marta extended her staff and swung it horizontally at Anánzu. Anánzu blocked it using her wooden staff with one hand. Marta attacked from behind and Anánzu blocked again. Then she followed through her swing and tripped Marta.

"Sorry," Marta apologized.

"Don't be. Attack me again." For the next couple of hours, Marta and Anánzu sparred using their staffs. As Marta slowly discovered, she did have the expert skills needed to use her staff and soon, she was swinging and twirling it like a professional. But Anánzu noticed that Marta was still lacking something, something that she desperately needed: the courage needed to use the skills. She had only seen this courage in one other individual and she... well... perhaps the raid on the terrorists' fortress will reveal this courage to Marta.

When their practice was over, Marta and Anánzu sat on a small hill. Anánzu's visible purple eye kept glancing over to Marta.

"Thank you again for rescuing me," Marta said unaware of Anánzu's repetitive gaze.

"It was my pleasure." She sighed, "You remind me so much of her."

"Huh, who?"

"My only daughter, Aleeta."

"Your daughter? But... you look so young!"

"Yes, and I was young when I had her." Anánzu got a far-off look. "My father was rather insistent about continuing the family line. Back then, we were always under attack by one enemy or another. He wanted to know that the leadership of the Riders of Tch'Kar would be protected in case we were to die in battle.

"My father married me off to a childhood friend. Everybody, even us, knew that we were too young but things were just that uncertain back then. It was not long after that I gave birth. My husband perished from the heat while on a mission in Estrellia.

Aleeta was my only remaining link to him, as he had no living family of his own."

"I can't believe it!"

"Believe it, Meina Utar, as I said before, my father was insistent about continuing the line. His orders that I marry and bare a child were harsh, but I could tell that he truly loved me and I tried to express and equal level of love to Aleeta."

Marta wondered about her own father, did he feel about her the same way Anánzu felt about Aleeta? Was that why he was so hard on her, because he actually loved her? It seemed so unlikely and yet it was the most logical answer.

"Aleeta was always so lively, so full of life and love. She believed that the Guardians instilled good in everyone and that evil was resulted when good intentions clashed. She always played the peacemaker when an argument broke out. As I told you before, the other Riders listened to her despite her age. She was after all, descended from their leader. She was about your age when…"

"When what?" Marta saw that Anánzu was about to cry so she dropped the subject. "Never mind, you don't have to tell me."

But Anánzu, knowing she couldn't ignore history forever, continued it. "We were attacked one night, while we slept. One of my Riders betrayed us to the enemy. My father and I were able to get away, but… they got her. They attacked her mercilessly." Anánzu wiped a tear from her visible eye. "When my father and I returned, we saw her… naked, skin already growing white, tied to a tree like she was some sort of animal." Anánzu closed her eye. "I never slept peacefully from that day on. That was about six years ago."

"I'm sorry for your lost," Marta said. She told Anánzu of how she lost her parents and Gerard. When she thought about it, she and Anánzu had a lot in common. They both lost people important to them; their belief that everything was righteous and true was shattered, as are the case with most children going through a tragedy.

Anánzu was overcome with emotions. She placed her hand over her visible eye so that Marta couldn't see her tears. But Marta, in an act of reassurance, took Ananzu's pale hand in both of hers and squeezed it gently.

"I know I'm not Aleeta, but... I promise I'll help you get back at the evil Riders of Tch'Kar. They took something from both of us, your daughter and my friend. And I promise they'll pay for all their crimes."

Anánzu smiled. "Marta, you are very courageous, perhaps even more so than me."

"No, I'm not," Marta said looking away ashamed. "I'm a selfish little girl who's thought of nothing but taking revenge on the people who destroyed my village."

"And that is what makes you courageous you're willing to do immediately what I, in the many years since that fateful day, could not. And for showing me a possible future for myself, I am grateful." Anánzu touched two fingers to Marta's forehead and said "May the Guardians' light shine down upon you." Marta beamed for that was considered the ultimate blessing, normally only used by the Sages but others have been known to use it when they really trusted and respected one another.

Anánzu was grateful that she had found a kindred spirit in Marta. Anánzu meant every word of what she said, every tear was genuine. Marta trusted her, and she was grateful of that, it was like the Guardians chose to bring Aleeta back to life through Marta. She only hoped Marta doesn't suffer the same fate as Aleeta.

"Anánzu." Anánzu opened her eye. Jeffrey was standing before her. Marta had fallen asleep at her side. The sun's position had changed showing some time had passed. Jeffrey cast his eyes to the edge of the forest. Anánzu gently laid Marta down and followed him to the edge.

"Anánzu, I fear that you are investing too much time in the Iberians." Anánzu was silent so Jeffrey continued. "You shouldn't become too attached to them, for we are bound to part ways after this next mission."

"True," she agreed. "But if all goes well, there won't be any more missions after this."

"A warrior can not get too attached to another. Do you recall what happened last time?"

"I remember, but the Guardians will not let history repeat it self."

"Blast it, Anánzu, distance yourself from the Iberian girl before you suffer again!"

Anánzu grabbed Jeffrey's neck. Despite her frame, she was strong. "Are you ordering me?"

"N... no," Jeffrey gagged. "I am just trying to spare you more heartache."

Anánzu dropped him. "The relationship between the Iberian girl and I is none of your business. We have both suffered hardships and both had to endure. When the time comes to part ways, I will deal with it in my own fashion but only when that time comes. Have you forgotten that such disdainful behavior is what caused the Riders of Tch'Kar to be split in two? I will not let another exodus like that happen again."

"Anánzu..."

"You have made your point, now leave my sight."

Jeffrey sighed. "Just remember that I warned you." And he left, Ananzu stared at her feet. "It is more than resemblance," she argued with herself. "There is something about them. Guardians, what are you trying to tell me?" The sun had set so that it was directly behind Marta, casting its light like it was solely meant for her. "I wonder," Anánzu muttered. She looked from the sleeping Marta to the sun. "The sun is setting, it is time." She woke Marta and then gathered the rest of the Iberians and her own troops to discuss their plan of attack. "We shall attack at nightfall. Since it's a moonless night, there will be no illumination to reveal us," Ananzu said to her Riders of Tch'Kar and the Iberians. "We'll need to use a hook and chain to scale the wall of their fortress. Once there, we will clear the guards using weapons and magic. After that, Maran will seek out Ada and rescue her. In the mean time, we will send most of our forces to engage the main forces of the evil Riders. Every last one of them will be slaughtered, only then will our name be cleared."

"The evil Riders are very bloodthirsty," Sage Mattonda pointed out. "There is a chance that many of your forces will be killed."

"We have been waiting our entire lives for this moment," Anánzu said as she removed her kimono. Underneath it, she wore a silver breast plate connected by two silver-colored leather straps. She put on silver arm and leg guards and donned a helmet with a unicorn head on the front. One of the other Riders gave her a longbow and quiver of silver arrows. "Win or lose, this shall be our greatest hour. Come, we move out!" Everybody got on horses and took off towards the evil Riders' fortress.

As Anánzu predicted, the moonless night shielded their approach. The guards stationed around the outer wall were almost suspiciously minimal. Anánzu and several archers fired their arrows and quickly took out the guards stationed there. They then moved up to the wall. One of the Anánzu's Riders of Tch'Kar, a muscular man named Koshack who could create anything with his mind (but only at the risk of lowering his life span), threw the hook onto the wall and the Iberians, Anánzu, and twelve of her soldiers, including Koshack, climbed up the chain.

Once on the keep, they silently made their way down to the ground. There were few guards around the courtyard. Marta gathered some energy and prepared to release it while the Sage's staff and Daniel's talisman began powering up. But Anánzu pushed her way to the front and cocked her bow. She fired a glowing arrow. Maran heard her mutter the word 'multiply' and the one arrow became five. Each of the arrows struck one of the guards and they fell down.

"This is almost too easy," Andros commented in a suspicious tone. Marta found his pessimism irritating. The Iberians and Anánzu dashed across the courtyard to the inner bailey. Sage Mattonda used his staff to blast a hole in the wall. "Maran, find Ada," he instructed. The ghost turned invisible and went through the bailey to find her. He returned only moments later.

"I found her," he reported. "But she's being guarded."

"How many guards are there?" Sage Mattonda asked.

"Only two but they look pretty strong."

"Let's go," Daniel said just before taking off down a spiral staircase that was to the left of the opening. The others soon followed but Anánzu's troops decided to hold back and stave off any reinforcements that might come their way. They arrived at the dungeon. Two guards, one on each side, were standing next to a door. Anánzu took aim with her bow and fired a silver arrow. "Pierce," was the command she used and just like that, the arrow went straight through one of the guard's sides. Andros threw a small vine on the ground and it grew and wrapped itself around the other guard so tight that it knocked him out.

Andros knelt by the lock and took out a pick. "This will only take a moment to..." A blast from Daniel's talisman shattered the door into splinters. He ran inside followed by Sage Mattonda, Marta, Maran, and Anánzu. "Blow to pieces," Andros grunted and put his pick away and casually went inside.

They couldn't believe their eyes. Ada was crumpled up on a shelf-like bed, beaten to a pulp. Her clothes were tattered almost to the point where they were barely hanging on her body. She had a black eye and bloody lip and a blue spot on her arm.

"Ada!" Daniel shouted running up to her.

"Hold still," Sage Mattonda instructed. He stuck the pointed end of his staff into her energy chains and they disintegrated.

Ada slowly opened her eyes. They were bloodshot and had bags underneath them. She looked up at Daniel. "Daniel? Daniel, it's you!" She cried into his shoulder.

"You can cry your eyes out later," Andros said. "Right now, we need to get out of here." Sage Mattonda handed his staff to Captain Garan and picked Ada up, wrapping her in Marta's cape, graciously donated.

"Anánzu," said a voice. Everyone pounded up the stairs to find out that Ananzu's men had been cornered. In the courtyard, over the dead bodies of the rest of Ananzu's soldiers, were the evil Riders of Tch'Kar.

"I had a feeling this would be a trap," Andros muttered as he readied his daggers.

"So, my dear, we meet again," Zachariah said evilly. "Even without our informant, it was child's play to decrypt your plan of attack."

"What informant?" Anánzu asked.

"You should've listened to me, Anánzu," Jeffrey said stepping from a crowd of evil Riders. "It could've saved you from heartache."

"You traitorous, dishonorable, piece of worthless excuse for a man," Anánzu insulted cocking her bow and aiming at him. "I'll strike you in two!"

"Temper, temper," Zachariah said wagging his finger. "You wouldn't want my friends to get upset, would you?" Archers and swordsmen aimed their weapons at the group.

"I have had enough of these miscreants," Sage Mattonda said passing Ada off to Captain Garan and taking his staff. The orb on top of the staff began glowing immensely. "Feel the power of the Sages!" Sage Mattonda threw his staff into the air and it came down in the center of the large crowd of evil Riders. A bubble of energy formed around the staff and expanded. Evil Riders began flying as the bubble hit them. "Marta, quickly gather as much energy as you can and release it directly in front of you. We'll support you."

"I'll try, my Sage," Marta said. The others protected Marta from advancing enemy troops while she began her dance. The dance took over a minute before Marta could hold no more and cried out, "Vibro-shock," before releasing it. The shock wave force plowed through evil Riders like a stampeding buffalo.

Anánzu marveled at the actions of the Iberians. Despite only being together for a couple of days, they were just as efficient as she was with her troops. They were so strong and brave, and they were the only ones who didn't know it. Anánzu suddenly saw Marta's head glow a golden color. The same was for Daniel, Andros, Maran, and even Ada. Anánzu had an epiphany. Were they the ones? Were they the Utars, the Legendaries? Were they the group that was destined to carry on their work? They had to be, all the evidence said so. On the surface, Anánzu couldn't believe it, but deep down, she knew it was true. They were the Utars and no matter the cost, they must survive, even if it meant her life. Anánzu lost a daughter to them; she didn't want any more innocents to suffer the same fate.

The Iberians along with Ada, Anánzu, and her remaining troops ran towards the center of the evil Riders but the evil Riders surrounded them.

"There's no way any of you will leave here alive," Zachariah said as he summoned his own magic, a sphere of lava with devastating properties. "Prepare to fire!"

"You're wrong," Anánzu said. "Someone will leave." She turned to Sage Mattonda. The two locked eyes for what seemed like a long time. Then they both nodded, each knowing what was going to happen.

Anánzu turned to the kids. "It's up to you."

"What do you mean it's up to us?" Andros asked.

"The key to saving Tel-ána lies with you. Even if we don't survive, you must."

"Don't survive?" Maran's eyes widened. "You don't mean..."

Anánzu nodded. "We will hold them out for as long as possible. You must get out of here."

"You must come with us," Captain Garan pleaded. "You can help us in our quest!"

"We have been ready since birth to die in battle," one of Anánzu's Riders said. "We have no remorse or fears about dying."

"In fact, we'd rather die than retreat like cowards," another added.

"No, we're all going or nobody's going," Marta said with tears in her eyes. She had come to respect Anánzu in the short time they met. She had all the courage and ferocity of her father and the wisdom and kindness of her mother.

Anánzu smiled. She remembered when she was like that, righteous and noble. But what's more, the way Marta acted; it was the same way Aleeta usually acted before Anánzu went on a supply raid, all righteous and compassionate for her. She leaned down and kissed Marta on the cheek. "Irndo win vi, meina Utar," she whispered into Marta's ear. Marta froze, she didn't recognize what the words were, but she knew the language was one of the ancient ones that were used by the Sages and one other group, though Marta couldn't remember what that group was.

"It's time!" Sage Mattonda cried. He slammed his staff down into the ground. A crack began to form around them. Anánzu fired one of her silver arrows. "Multiply!" The one arrow became seven and each one struck an evil Rider. Her surviving soldiers each drew a sword or went into close quarters combat.

The ground underneath the Iberians and Ada began rising. Sage Mattonda covered them in a shield from those who could fire projectiles at them.

Marta made one last attempt to call Anánzu. "Anánzu, please come with us!"

Anánzu looked up and smiled. She knew that the safety of Telána was in good hands. Marta, I am truly glad to have met you.

The Guardians have indeed chosen to reincarnate Aleeta for me. Anánzu took out her last silver arrow and aimed it at the ground. "Aleeta, I'm coming to join you, please wait for me," she muttered. She launched the arrow and called out, "massive eruption!"

"Anánzu, no!" Jeffrey cried. But sure enough, the entire courtyard was engulfed in a huge fireball.

"NO!" Marta screamed at the top of her lungs as the slab of ground they were floating on drifted away from the fortress.

That night, the group rested at a small clearing. Sage Mattonda's staff was healing Ada. Most of the others were already asleep. Marta was still crying over the lost of Anánzu and the Riders of Tch'Kar.

Sage Mattonda came up to her. "Marta, you must sleep. We have a long journey ahead of us."

"I'm sorry, My Sage," Marta apologized. "But... it feels like I just lost another parent. I know we only knew Anánzu for a brief time, but... I..." A new wave of tears threatened to overtake her.

"Marta, please understand that Anánzu and her soldiers were ready to die. Please take comfort in knowing that she died in the most noblest of causes."

"My... my Sage, what does 'irndo win vi, meina Utar' mean?"

Sage Mattonda looked at her surprised. Then he replied, "It's an ancient language used by the Sages. It means 'Go with victory, my little Legendary.'"

"What's a Legendary?" Marta questioned.

"The Utar, or Legendaries, were the first Sages, who oversaw the forming of Tel-ána's twelve kingdoms. Back then, a lot of people were opposed to joining a particular kingdom, said they wanted to remain independent. Some even went so far as to attack one another like savages. The Utar not only defeated them, but convinced a majority of them to favor the forming of the twelve kingdoms. Their work was so abnormal that it is said that the Guardians themselves anointed them upon their deaths as their honor guard. That's why they're called Legendaries."

"Anánzu… she called me a little Utar."

Sage Mattonda smiled. "Consider that an immense compliment. It means she thinks you're destined for greatness. Now, little one, it's time for you to sleep." Sage Mattonda touched her head with his hands and rubbed it. Marta immediately fell into a trance. She fell onto Sage Mattonda's lap. "When you awake, you will be renewed," he said as he gently laid her on the ground and covered her in a blanket. He got up and went deep into the forest. Only about twelve meters outside of the camp, he stopped. He reached into the darkness and yanked out a scrawny-looking man with a hook for a hand. "Have they been disposed of?" He asked.

"Yes, sire," the man replied. "We dumped them over a cliff. Only birds of prey would be able to find them."

"Good. Make sure they don't become a nuisance again. I must go to Kashuto but I will send word when I want to begin the next phase of the plan."

"Of course, sire, but…" Sage Mattonda motioned him to continue. "Sire, some of the others are getting… well… irritated. They've done what you asked, but they haven't seen anything in return."

"Reassure them that once I am in power, they will get the riches they desire."

"Yes, sire." The hooked man left and Sage Mattonda went back to the camp unaware that Maran was spying on him. Maran wondered what Sage Mattonda was doing talking to a man whom Maran recognized as a member of the evil Riders of Tch'Kar. Was the Iberian Sage a part of the evil Riders? Maran was afraid to come to that conclusion because if the Sage found out that he accused him, or that he knew, he might imprison him or do something even worse. He had to keep his mouth shut for now.

Mishanko had no mountain ranges but it did have a large canyon near its western boarder. Thermal air had been known to rise up though records did exist that said that the canyon did have a bottom. It was one of Tel-ána's mysterious wonders, much like the Temple of Maran in Iberia. It did have a bottom and it was there that several bodies were dumped. The bodies lay strewn about. The hand of one of the bodies was formed into a fist.

Kashuto rests on the northern coastline of Tel-ána and is one of the smaller kingdoms. Nestled between Costal Glen and Estrellia, Kashuto serves as primarily a trading post between Pasornin, also called the island nation, and the rest of the Tel-ána kingdoms. It was also, unfortunately, the source of all shady dealings in Tel-ána. However, its ruler, Regent Quinton Kashu the IV, pays no attention to it. This is because most of the time, the shady dealings did not involve Kashuto or put it in danger. In fact, Kashuto profited and prospered from the subterfuge that took place within its boarders and sovereignty prevented other kingdoms from intervening.

Sage Mattonda and the others arrived at the boarder of Kashuto through Barrel Pass. As the name suggests, the pass was so narrow that, had it been round, it would've been mistaken for a cannon barrel. Thieves had been known to ambush people through the pass where there was no escape, which was why they were traveling swiftly. Their horses kicked up dust along the dry road. Overhead, Maran kept a keen eye out for anybody on the cliffs.

"My Sage," Marta called. "How much longer until we get through the pass?"

"Not far," Sage Mattonda replied. "I can see the mouth now." The pass began to expand a little until it opened up entirely. They were immediately in a forest. The trees there were huge, probably bigger than most castles.

"So how do we find this Harold guy?" Andros asked. "King Adleton said he lived on the north coast but the north coast is very vast."

"He lives in a tower overlooking a cape northeast of Barrel Pass," Ada explained though it sounded like she was reciting from a script.

Andros gave her an odd look. "And just how do you know where he lives?"

"Harold is an old friend of the family. He has been my tutor ever since I was old enough to hold up a book."

"So is his wisdom reliable?" Captain Garan questioned.

"I have had no reason to doubt him before," Ada said like it was an act of defiance to Captain Garan's question. "I see no reason to doubt him now."

"Then let's go." The group ran until they could hear the ocean splashing up against the coast. They could smell the salt tinted air and feel the cool breeze on their skin.

"It's so beautiful," Marta gasped. Clearly, she had never seen the ocean before nor had Daniel.

"My father used to bring me here during the warm seasons when I was very young," Ada commented. "In some strange way, it always brought me peace." Marta permitted herself a smile as she felt a warm breeze caress her cheek. Daniel noticed it and was glad. It has been a long time since he has seen his cousin smile for real. Not since before the destruction of their village has he seen her truly smile. It reminded him that she was still the fun-loving girl whom he used to play Search with all those years ago (The kids, eager to separate themselves from her, made her the searcher and she had to find all of them). Granted, the two of them had to do some fast growing since then. He hasn't even had the luxury of mourning for the lost of his family and friends. But he also wondered what would happen to him after all this was over? What would happen to Marta? Would they stay together or would they be separated? Daniel hated that idea, the idea that he would be separated from the only family he had left. And who would take them in until they came of age? By societal laws, they were too old to be adopted yet too young to live on their own. Maybe King Gladirus would take them in, or maybe they would they be sent to another village, maybe in another kingdom? Part of Daniel even entertained the notion that Ada would invite them to stay at the Morbian palace as servants. True the work would be grueling and the pay next to nothing but at least they would have a place to call home.

The vast blue sea was more beautiful than anything Marta had ever seen before. Water as far as the eye could see, disappearing into the horizon. It was hard to tell where the sea ended and the sky began. Marta could see why Ada would find peace with it. The sea seemed to be never-changing. Like even after they all grow old and die, the sea would still be there, caressing the unworthy shore with its waves. It made her feel… reassured.

Sage Mattonda's staff started to glow, a sign that they were in danger. Bandits revealed themselves from behind them. But they weren't normal bandits, Daniel was sure of that. They were the evil Riders of Tch'Kar. Seeing them infuriated Marta. They were the ones who brutally attacked Ada, the ones who, in the same brutal manner, killed Anánzu and her Riders of Tch'Kar. Marta took out her metal pole and batted a bandit's head with it, using the skills that Anánzu taught her. She repeated this attack with three more bandits. This is for you, Anánzu.

Ada transformed into a wingless dragon and started swatting bandits like flies. She also breathed fire on them. Captain Garan and Sage Mattonda were striking them with their weapons.

It was then that Andros knew something odd about the bandits. "Hey, these guys are all the same!" It was true. They all had the same face, same hair, and same build. Only their clothing varied. They... or rather he was a mashyyk or multiplier, someone who could make copies of himself. Marta tried to remember what her father taught her about multipliers. She remembered him telling her that mashyyk copies were invincible. They could be knocked down, but not killed. But the original was not invincible. If the original could be found and defeated, the copies would disappear. The problem was she couldn't tell the difference. But she knew someone who could.

"Daniel," Marta called. "Use your foresight to find the original!" Daniel's eyes glowed blue as he looked around. All the bandits that Ada, Andros, Marta, Sage Mattonda, and Captain Garan were fighting had faint light-blue outlines. That meant they were all copies. "I can't find him!"

"Then get higher, idiot," Andros snapped.

"How do I do that?"

"Daniel, hop on," Ada called as she sprouted a set of wings. Daniel climbed onto her large scaly back and Ada the dragon raised herself into the air. She flew in a circular pattern around the battlefield.

Daniel used his foresight to scan the area around them. Daniel finally spotted him by the dark blue outline and white skeleton hiding behind a tree south-east of their current location. Ada flew down and plowed into him. He smashed his head against a tree and was killed almost instantly. Immediately, the copies disappeared.

"Well done, Daniel," Sage Mattonda congratulated as the two returned to their party. "And you too, Ada."

"Thank you, My Sage," Daniel said.

"Yes, thank you," Ada joined in.

"Something tells me that those are the bandits that kidnapped Ada and finished off Anánzu's Riders," Andros guessed. Marta scowled at the young thief's never-ending pessimism and the dismissal tone he used in talking about their one-time, but true ally. But deep down, she knew he was right.

"I'm afraid we can't waste time on speculation," Sage Mattonda said. "Until we get to Harold's Tower, we're still at a disadvantage. We must continue."

The group continued along the coastline. Turning northeast, they continued along the coast until a faint cylindrical object appeared in the distance.

"That's it," Ada confirmed. "That's Harold's Tower." But the group only proceeded 200 more yards before a giant monster burst from the sand. It had a flat frog-like head and a burly body. Its four legs ended in webbed feet with three sharp claws.

"A Drolkrik," Sage Mattonda realized.

"I thought they only inhabited marshes and swamps," Captain Garan said. "And I have never seen one that huge before."

"Let's get it," Andros said like a war cry. He drew his dagger but Ada stepped in front and blocked his advance with her arms.

"Wait, it's friendly!" She protested.

"Are you crazy?" Andros asked.

Ada just turned towards the Drolkrik. "Hello, Mikaelo, do you remember me?" She greeted the Drolkrik like she was talking to someone younger than her, like around four or five years.

"Mikaelo?" Andros almost snickered. Mikaelo's head lowered to Ada's level. Its tongue slithered out and touched Ada's outstretched hand. It slid its tongue along Ada's body. Marta shivered in disgust.

"Drolkriks have no nose," Sage Mattonda explained. "But they can sense someone familiar through their tongue the same way dogs do through their smell."

Mikaelo's tongue retracted into its head. It nuzzled up against her. Ada laughed and patted the Drolkrik's nose, or rather the region where the nose would be. "I'm glad to see you too, boy," she said. "Go tell Uncle Harold we're here." Mikaelo dove back under the sand.

"And just how do you know that thing?" Andros asked putting away his dagger. Ada explained that Mikaelo is Harold's pet and bodyguard. Whenever he came over to teach her, he would bring the Drolkrik along. Ada would often play with him. He actually used to be normal Drolkrik size (20 inches) but something in the sea water made him grow abnormally huge. Harold's magic, mental communication with animals; enabled him to tame the massive Drolkrik.

Ada and the others reached the tower without any further predicament. A man with wrinkled skin, a thin moustache, white tufts of hair, and a white smock came out.

"Uncle Harold!" Ada cried running up to him and embracing him fiercely.

"Adora, what a surprise," Harold said. "And you brought friends too. Well come in, come in."

The tower was much less than they expected it to be. Upon first glance, it appeared simple: just a kitchen and a sleeping hammock. The only window was half-way between ground level and the top of the tower.

"Now, what can I do for you?" Harold asked.

"Uncle Harold, Marta and Daniel live in the Iberian Kingdom. Their village was destroyed and they want to find out who did it and why. I thought that since..."

Harold hushed her. He looked around before gesturing, "Follow me." Harold opened up a trap door and ushered everyone down.

The hidden room that Harold revealed looked like it was bigger than the tower. It was definitely roomier. The wall was made of solid stone. In addition to tables of various artifacts, there were several tubes that lead into the ground, a niche with a bookshelf, and even a table with scientific instruments on it. Sage Mattonda could feel a strange magic around it. He hypothesized that the magic field prevented oracles, telepaths, people with foresight like Daniel, and other people with such magic from finding it.

Harold confirmed his theory once they were all down. "Forgive my curtness; if certain authoritative parties found out what I did, it would be all over for me and my business. Now, explain it to me again."

"Marta and Daniel's village was destroyed and they want to find out who did it and why. Since you're connected with the Necromon, I was hoping you could find out through your connections."

Harold put on a stern face. "What you're asking is a very tall order, Adora."

"Please, Uncle Harold, I know you can do it."

"Well... I'm not making any promises that I'll find anything, but I'll see what I can do."

Ada's eyes shone. "Oh thank you, Uncle Harold!"

Harold's assuring smile returned. He patted her hair. "Anything for you, my dear; in the mean time, make yourselves comfortable. My home is your home."

Captain Vostock stood guard outside the Kashuto end of Barrel Pass. He couldn't believe that bloated fool Garan gave him the slip. And he had the best trackers in all of Tel-ána with him. He was going to relish in torturing that obese Captain and killing the other Iberians.

Vostock's anger with the Iberians may be excessive, but it is sound. He had lost more friends than he could count to Iberian blades and magic. One of his good friends, Jason, was even killed by a Sage when a Morbian platoon attempted to storm the Iberian capitol during the war. King Adleton said he wanted his daughter back no matter his cost. Of course, he wasn't about to disobey his own king, he would get Princess Adora back, but King Adleton didn't clearly state the conditions of the Iberians which, to Vostock, was the same as condemning them to death.

"Captain Vostock!" The scout that he sent ahead had returned. "They've been through here, sir. One of our best Windwakers confirmed it through his link with nature."

"Good. Everyone move out, we will make camp along the coast line."

Unaware of the proximity of Vostock and his soldiers, Ada and the others rested at Harold's place. Actually, Marta, Daniel, and Captain Garan rested. Maran explored Harold's underground workshop and Andros and Sage Mattonda kept a close eye on Ada as Harold explained to them about the Tel-ána Necromon.

"Some people just don't like authority," Harold flat-out stated. "They believe that there is too much authority limiting the freedoms of the common people. So they have formed an underground organization where they do whatever they want to do to whomever they want to do it to."

"That's horrible," Ada gasped.

"True. I will not attempt to defend their actions, but the members of the Necromon also keep a close watch on each other not only to cover each other's back, but simply because they don't fully trust one another. One must keep their friends close and their enemies closer. With my communication tubules, I can receive and relay information to anyone in the Necromon."

"And why do they trust you?" Sage Mattonda asked.

"They don't, but my information has never been misguided before, so they have no reason to try to kill me. So tell me Ada, how did you convince your father to let you leave the palace?"

As Ada explained her story and what was happening, Sage Mattonda slipped away. He went up to Maran and whispered, "Keep an eye on Harold, there is something about him that worries me." Without questioning why, Maran nodded and went over to listen to Harold and Ada's conversation.

Sage Mattonda explored Harold's book shelf. If Harold was connected with the Tel-ána Necromon, then he just might have The Book. The Book is an ancient text, even older than the Guardian Journals. From what he remembered from his own Sage's teachings, The Book contained spells for utilizing what is known as raw magic, extremely powerful and versatile magic that was said to be the first magic used on Tel-ána, after the Guardians bestowed upon the people their power and knowledge. Raw magic was so powerful that it overwhelmed all other magic, including protection magic, like the one that protected the Morbian Guardian Journal from being duplicated. Sage Mattonda wanted... no, needed The Book if he was to make his plan a success. The problem was the Council of Sages had tried vehemently to publicly act like The Book didn't even exist. Anybody who stepped forward claiming to have a copy of The Book would be either branded a liar or "mysteriously vanishes" and everyone acting like they never even heard of the person. But Sage Mattonda knew the truth, The Book did exist, and an underground spy like Harold would have all kinds of texts that have been banded by the Council of Sages and Tel-ána authorities including The Book.

He finally found it. The Book was an old, dusty text bound by a leather cover. The pages were so delicate that they could probably crumble if someone even breathed on it. Sage Mattonda skimmed through it until he found, in the original language of the Guardians, the magic spell he was seeking. But there was something else with it: a warning at the beginning.

Beware the use of Raw magic. For doing so will summon a power older than the Guardians. Chaos will erupt and the land will be torn. The Utars and the Guardians shall fight until peace balances across the land.

"A power older than the Guardians," Sage Mattonda mumbled. Such an idea was ridiculous in his opinion. There is nothing more powerful or older than the Guardians. In fact, that was the key factor in his plan. He secretly pocketed the journal inside his robes.

Sage Mattonda returned to where the others were. "Get some rest," he told Ada and Andros.

"I think one of us should stay up," Andros suggested. "In case Harold tries anything."

"I understand your fear," Sage Mattonda said with emphasis, like he wasn't just talking about Harold. "But we will all need our strength," he added. "If we are to survive tomorrow's battle."

"You think there's going to be a battle?" Andros asked ignoring the chill he got when the Sage said, "I understand your fear."

"You saw the battle today. The Evil Riders of Tch'Kar are still out there, and they most likely want revenge on us for what happened at their fortress. We'll need all our wits about us if we're going out again."

Andros sighed. The Sage was right and, he hated to admit it, he was tired. He lay down and went to sleep.

The next day, while everyone was eating breakfast upstairs in the tower, Harold came up from the underground station. "My friends, I have disturbing news."

"Uncle Harold, what's wrong?" Ada asked.

"I have consulted several of my sources in the Necromon and while I have received no information on the circumstances regarding the destruction of the Iberian village, my sources have told me that someone is out to murder the Iberian King, Gladirus."

Everyone, even Andros, gasped. "Are you sure about this?" Sage Mattonda asked.

Harold nodded. "The specifics are sketchy to say the least, but someone is definitely after King Gladirus' life. They most likely want to overthrow him and usurp his kingdom."

"Perhaps whoever is out to kill King Gladirus also had a hand in destroying Gerard," Daniel said to Marta. "It's possible that the mastermind of all this wanted you to kill King Gladirus so he or she could take over."

"Or perhaps the village was destroyed to tarnish King Gladirus' reputation," Harold threw in. "Either way, it would be a perfect set-up for an overthrow."

"I can't sit like this!" Captain Garan cried. "I must be at my King's side."

"No," Sage Mattonda snapped. "I'll return to Iberia and warn King Gladirus. You all must continue to search for the truth. Do not forget, our original mission was to discover the circumstances behind the destruction of Gerard. I am a Sage; I will protect the King from this murderer."

"And just how will you get back?" Andros asked. "Iberia must be a week's journey from here."

"You just let me worry about that. You all worry about discovering the truth. Harold, please watch over them until they leave."

"Of course I will, Sage."

Sage Mattonda nodded and left the tower. Once outside, he held his staff high in the air and transformed into a beam of light. He shot up into the air and disappeared.

"I guess we should figure out what our next move is," Andros said.

"The Council," Marta muttered drawing glances from the others. "We must consult the Council of Sages."

Andros let out a harsh laugh. "Sure, and after that, we can go resurrect the Guardians," he said sarcastically. Visiting the Council of Sages was next to impossible because the chambers resided in a dimension apart from Tel-ána. Only Sages or those in-training to be a Sage could access it.

"Look, thief, you've been acting snide ever since we started this journey! Why can't you just accept things as they come and not retort every step someone makes? Why do you have to doubt everything including the obvious?" Andros was quiet. He mentally told himself that he didn't have to answer the question; he owed nothing to the Iberian Captain or these children. He only hoped that everyone would take his silence as a signal to change the subject.

However, the exact opposite happened as Marta put what was just said together with what he said at the Inn back in Iberia. "It's got something to do with the scar," she deduced. "Someone you trusted betrayed you, maybe even gave you that scar over your eye. Now because of that event, you don't trust anybody, even those who have proven to be your allies."

"Don't talk about things you don't understand," Andros argued.

"But that's just it," Marta came back. "I do understand! Somebody in my own kingdom destroyed my village. My village was betrayed by the Iberian army. By all rights, I should be like you, moody and doubtful over everything someone says. But I'm not, in fact, I'm just the opposite. Being betrayed actually made me more trusting, especially towards strangers like Anánzu because, as it turned out, strangers can be trustworthy even when people you know are not! Ada, Maran, Captain Garan, even Anánzu and her Riders of Tch'Kar, all of them were originally strangers but

HAROLD RAY

have proven they could be trusted." Daniel, Ada, and Maran were impressed with Marta's speech, especially her passion.

Andros, however, wasn't impressed. "And that's why that, when you are betrayed, it will make the hurt worst than it would if you didn't trust them," he said harshly. "I hope I'm around to see it just so I can tell you 'I told you so.'" With those words, Andros dropped to Harold's underground chambers. Andros might as well have slapped Marta in the face because that's what his words felt like, a sting across the cheek. She actually touched her cheek like it just been slapped.

"As rude as he was," Daniel said clearing his throat. "Andros does have a point. It's going to be very hard to get an audience with the Council of Sages, even more so than it was trying to get an audience with King Gladirus."

"Sage Petro often told me that to get to the Council of Sages, you must first be invited by a Sage," Ada informed them.

"And that chance just left a while ago," Daniel commented referring to Sage Mattonda.

"Go see Sage Kimo in Costal Glen," Harold instructed. "He is very benign; he would most likely grant your request."

"All right, let's get ready," Marta said. As she started to pack up the few things she had, Harold laid a hand on her shoulder. "Andros's logic behind being betrayed is sound, but I do not believe he meant to turn it into a personal attack against you. Do not hate him."

"I don't know," Marta simply replied. "I just don't know."

Andros plopped down on the floor near Harold's bookshelf. Marta's words were still ringing in his ears.

"Someone you trusted betrayed you."

"I do understand; my own village was betrayed by the Iberian army. By all rights, I should be like you."

"Being betrayed actually made me more trusting."

"She's wrong," Andros said pulling his knees up against his chest. "Nobody can be trusted. Everyone has the capacity for deception. It's just... natural."

"Andros, it's time to leave," Maran informed as he floated through the ceiling. "Are you going to leave with us or go back on your own?"

Andros smiled hard and rose. "It's not like I have any choice," he told the ghost. "If I don't come with you guys, King Gladirus will have me hunted down and tortured severely."

"Oh," Maran simply replied as he floated back through the ceiling. Andros actually felt sorry for the ghost. From what Daniel told him, Maran has no memory of his past and had never left the Temple where his body was buried. He's probably the only one with a decent excuse for his naiveté. Andros climbed back up the ladder. Once there, he joined the others. When he and Marta set eyes on each other, they both froze, both faces expressing neutral expressions. The others were afraid that a battle was about to break out. Then Andros said, "Let's go."

Sage Mattonda materialized in Sage Petro's chambers once again. To his amazement, the Guardian Journal was still on the shelf where he left it. There was no indication that security had been increased since his last visit. Was he really able to slip under Sage Petro's senses so quickly? The Morbian Sage's abilities were obviously not as acute as most were.

Sage Mattonda took the Guardian Journal and placed it on the table. He then placed the Book over it. He then aimed his staff at it.

"Karos dodu de whan, parkos nea dupla estu song!" Sage Mattonda recited the incantation to merge the raw magic of The Book with the duplication spell he tried earlier. The Guardian Journal started to glow. Energy transferred to another place on the table. Sage Mattonda utilized all his magical dexterity to complete

HAROLD RAY

the spell. There was a reason raw magic had been outlawed. That was because that using it actually tapped into the very life force of the person performing the spell. Using too much raw magic could cause the death of the spell caster.

Sage Mattonda took the duplicate Guardian Journal and skimmed through it to make sure all the pages had been copied. He then disappeared without returning the Guardian Journal to its original place.

"I wish you good luck, young ones," Harold said. "I'll try to gather more information then send it to you as it becomes available."

"Uncle Harold, thank you," Ada said hugging the old man. Harold returned the hug and then went back into his lighthouse.

"So I guess we're off to Costal Glen then," Daniel guessed.

"Wrong!" It was Captain Vostock, who appeared with his troops. "The only place you're going is to your death!"

"Captain Vostock, what's the meaning of this?" Ada demanded to know. "What business do you have here?"

"My Princess, we have come to liberate you from your barbaric captors," Vostock explained in a proud tone. He turned to the Iberians and his voice became sinister. "And you miserable ingrates shall pay for your crimes tenfold!"

"No, I won't have you attack them." Ada stood in between them. "Go back and tell my father that I'll return to Morbia when I'm good and ready."

"Princess, your father has ordered me to bring you home at any cost. Meaning he doesn't care about these miserable little wastes of breath."

Captain Garan drew his sword. "You children run, I'll hold them off as long as I can."

"No way," Andros said brandishing his dagger. "I'm going to give these slush-for-brains a beating they will never forget."

It was then that Harold came out. "Is everything all right? I heard some ruckus and thought... oh Captain Vostock, good afternoon."

"Harold," Vostock addressed pointing his sword threateningly at the old man. "You shall be punished for aiding these criminals."

"Captain Vostock, you may be a good soldier but you are terrible when it comes to politics," Harold said raising his glasses. "You can not punish me because you are not inside Morbia territory. If this was going on inside Nutros then you could kill me if you so wish. But you are a guest in Kashuto and there are a lot of people who would be upset if something were to happen to me including the Regent. You would have lit a match in a powder keg room metaphorically speaking." The patronizing tone in Harold's voice told the Iberians that he was used to Vostock's wild threats.

Vostock scowled. He could see that Harold had outwitted him politically. But the Iberians were another story. "Kill them! But don't harm the Princess." The guards charged the Iberians. Daniel and Andros were the first to act. Daniel unleashed a blast from his talisman that made two guards dive for cover. But before they could get up, Andros wrapped them up in vines.

Captain Vostock started to go after Daniel but a glitter of metal caught his eye. He quickly blocked Andros' dagger.

"Miserable little beggar," Vostock sneered turning on Andros.

"Pompous uptight blowhard," Andros countered taking out his other dagger. Captain Vostock quickly summoned his magic to turn invisible. He attacked Andros with several kids and knocked the boy down. He then did the same thing with Captain Garan and Marta.

"Daniel, hop on, I'll get us out of here." Ada commanded as she transformed into a winged horse. But as Daniel climbed on, something stabbed him in the shoulder. It was Andros' dagger, the one that he used against Captain Vostock. Daniel fell off of Ada and lost his talisman. Eyes shimmering with tears of pain, he crawled to retrieve the talisman. But Captain Vostock appeared, aiming his sword at the young boy's neck. "You shall be the first to die. I've seen how you've been eyeing my Princess. You miserable little commoner, you will pay for not showing her some respect."

Daniel watched in horror as Vostock raised his sword. He won't deny that Ada was good-looking, but Vostock was acting like even looking at her general direction was a violation punishable by death. Daniel braced for the contact of cold sharp steel.

"Daniel!" Marta cried.

"Vostock, don't do it!" Ada pleaded.

The sword started to come down.

"You touch one hair on their heads and I'll skewer you like the pig you are," a familiar voice said. The blade stopped literally two inches from Daniel's neck. Vostock cast his eyes to the right and saw that one of his armored knights was aiming a bow with a silver arrow cocked right at his head. Four more also had various weapons aimed at him and the remainder of his troops was surrounded by a small band of oddly-dressed warriors.

Marta couldn't believe her ears. "Anánzu, is that really you?" The visor on the knight holding the bow and arrow was lifted up and everyone could see that it was indeed Anánzu.

"Marta, you're looking well."

Marta started to run up to her but Andros put his arm out stopping her. "Wait a second, we all saw you destroyed back at the fortress of the terrorist Riders of Tch'Kar. How can you be alive?" He asked

"While it is true that some of us died, a majority of us managed to live," Anánzu explained. "One of us had the ability to place people into a death-like sleep which she activated in the midst of the explosion. Fortunately it was only temporary." The others were speechless at that revelation. Anánzu gave them an assuring smile.

HAROLD RAY

"The Guardians choose when to accept people into their Dimension and obviously, this was not our time to go."

"I'm so glad you're all right," Marta said this time breaking through Andros's barrier and running up to hug her mentor.

Anánzu smiled and placed a hand on Marta's head making her beam with pride. "I missed you too, meina Utar." She turned and scowled at Vostock. "Now, are we going to talk this out like civilized people or are you going to continue to be unreasonable?"

In the Iberian capitol, people were furiously storming towards Ricardo castle. Despite all efforts by the palace guard to retain them, they were quickly being overwhelmed. The people were chanting things like "Down with Gladirus!" and "Death to the tyrant!"

In his throne room, King Gladirus paced up and down. The rioting could be heard clearly outside. Suddenly a page ran into the throne room. His clothes were wrinkled and even torn in a couple of places. When he left ten minutes before, his clothes had been fine. "What's going on?" King Gladirus asked.

The page genuflected. "Your Highness, rioting has broken out in all the streets. Your guards are being overwhelmed! Even the army is beginning to take up arms against you." The boy's red face showed that he was ashamed to be the bearer of such bad news.

"Thank you, my boy," King Gladirus said. He took out some paper and began writing on it. "Take this to General Rore and tell him to head towards Vernaclia. As much as I hate to do it, we must ask for aide from other kingdoms."

"But Your Highness," the boy protested. "There are so many people blocking the main gate. How will I get out? I haven't even practiced using my magic yet."

King Gladirus smiled. "I have faith in you, my boy. That message may be the only thing that can restore balance and order in Iberia."

Suddenly the door burst open and twelve or so soldiers charged into the room. King Gladirus drew his sword. "Stay behind me, boy, these heretics shall not get either of us this day!"

"You have us mistaken, Your Highness," one of the guards said. They genuflected. "We're here to serve as your honor guard. We also bring information."

"What information?" King Gladirus asked lowering his sword.

"Sire, there is a rumor going around the capitol that it is your intention to initiate martial law and eventually enslave the people."

"That is absurd! Who would start such a rumor?"

"I have no idea, Your Highness," the guard admitted. "But that is what the people believe. They have decided to overthrow you before you could enact this scheme."

"I must speak to them, they must know that..." One of the windows burst open. As the shattering glass fell, flyers and wind wakers could be seen. They started to fly towards the window but hit a barrier set up by one of the guards using his magic.

"Your Highness, you must leave," the captain argued. "The people have devolved beyond reasoning and logic and can not be negotiated with and Gareth's shields can not hold for an indefinite amount of time."

"I will not leave. I prefer to face my accusers with pride and honor then to hide like a coward."

Another guard came bursting in. He quickly shut the doors and stuck his spear in between the handles. "They've penetrated the castle! They've penetrated the castle!"

"How?" The Captain asked.

"Some of the guards have joined the rebels," the guard explained. "Those who are loyal to King Gladirus could not hold them back. They stole several access spears and are now making their way here."

King Gladirus cursed. "Where is Sage Mattonda? His crystal must be telling him that there is danger to his kingdom so what happened to him?"

"I'm sorry, Your Highness, but I must insist on you retreating to a safe place for now. These rebels have murder on their minds. And with all due respect, sir, I would rather have you a fugitive than a corpse." The Captain persuaded.

King Gladirus nodded. Knowing that there were such devoted people near him assured him that everything was going to turn out all right. He ran over to a side wall and removed a brick to reveal a spike. He pricked his finger on the spike and allowed a single drop of blood to drip onto it. Bricks began moving until a small tunnel was revealed. King Gladirus turned to the pageboy. "Young boy, please listen to what I have to say. These may be the last instructions I will ever give." The pageboy looked like he was ready to cry. "I used to use this passageway to escape from my father when he was upset or spy on him when he had some important business to attend to. It leads to the army barracks. Give this message to General Rore than have him show you the Yumina passage. He will know what I'm talking about. Take it and head for Morbia."

"But Morbia's our enemy, aren't they?"

"Desperate times call for desperate measures." A tear dripped down the pageboy's cheek. King Gladirus embraced the boy like a son. "I need you to be strong boy, be strong for both of us. Please, do this for me."

The boy wiped away his tears and nodded smiling. "I'll do my best, Your Highness," he said.

"I know you will."

The pageboy got down on his hands and knees and crawled into the tunnel. As soon as he was out of sight, King Gladirus smiled and wiped the blood from the spike with his cape. The bricks slid back into place hiding the passageway.

"But Your Highness, what about you?" The Captain pointed out.

"Don't worry, Captain, There is more than one way to exit this throne room that doesn't involve death."

"They're here!" There was massive pounding on the doors. The guard's spear looked like it was ready to break. Gareth extended his other hand and set up a large forcefield leaving some guards trapped on the outside. These guards would fight the rebels until the bitter end. And judging from the pounding, the end will be very bitter. "The barrier will not hold them off for long."

"Just so it's long enough," the Captain replied.

"Captain," King Gladirus said. "Thank you. If everything turns out all right, I'll be sure to promote you."

The two clasped hands as the Captain said, "Our fathers served together under King Ricardo the V. Your father saved my father's life. It's the least I can do."

The doors burst open and a wave of angry people poured into the room. They began pounding on the barrier using physical force, magic, and weapons. Gareth grunted from the strain of having to set up two barriers. One was about to come down. King Gladirus ran over to his throne. As he did, he could hear the jeers from the people.

"You dirty rat!"

"Face us, you dishonorable old crone!"

"If you run, then you're guilty!"

"I will kill you!"

"I am sorry," King Gladirus simply replied. Sitting on his throne, he touched his ring to his palm. The ring that all Iberian kings were required to wear glowed and his throne began descending. As the throne disappeared, King Gladirus saw the front barrier fall and his allies struggling against the mob. No sooner had his throne fell into the shaft, a stone slab slid into place blocking the tunnel from the throne room.

King Gladirus took a deep breath. It would take a while for the throne to arrive at the tunnel deep underground. From there, a tunnel went underneath the moat and eventually leads outside the capitol.

"How," King Gladirus said to nobody. "How did things get so out of hand?"

That night, a bonfire was set up on the beach near Harold's lighthouse. It was too dangerous to travel at night and they needed to plan. Marta and Maran had informed Anánzu on what they learned and what they planned to do.

"I see," Anánzu muttered. "Well that certainly fits what I've learned."

"And what have you learned precisely?" Andros asked in his usual suspicious tone.

"We've learned that the evil Riders of Tch'Kar were responsible for the destruction of your village, Marta." Marta gasped. "Some of them impersonated Iberian soldiers and when King Gladirus ordered to quell the 'rebellion' in Gerard, they came along to perform as much destruction and devastation as possible, against the King's orders."

"You seem to know a lot," Andros said. "How do we know you're not part of the evil Riders? How do we know you're not responsible for the destruction of Gerard?"

"Stop that," Marta scolded slamming his shoulder. "Forgive Andros, he doesn't trust anybody."

"A good policy," Anánzu observed. "So here is the truth, whether you believe it or not, the truth is I got it straight from the mouth of our formal leader."

"How did you do that?" Maran asked.

Jeffrey looked over a map inside his tent. Word had finally come from the head man himself. Zachariah was sent to gather the remaining soldiers in Estrellia and press to Iberia through Morbia. This rouse was set up to think that Morbia decided to start another war between itself and Iberia.

Suddenly a dagger was lay against his throat. "Letting your guard down before a battle, Jeffrey, I thought I taught you better than that."

"Anánzu!" Anánzu quickly twirled him around and placed him against the table. "I thought…"

"You thought I was dead," Anánzu finished. "Maybe you should've spent more time with others than in your perverted books, otherwise you would've remembered Malos and how he can create the illusion of death." One of Jeffrey's hobbies was reading books that involved torture and the harming of others. He even had some that involved children being beaten up. It was the sickest form of literature in all of Tel-ána.

"No!" Jeffrey struggled to break free but Anánzu's grip was vice. "I suppose you intend to kill me."

"Oh, you would like that, wouldn't you? You would like to gain instant access to the Guardians' Dimension. Well I'm not letting you off that easy. You're going to answer a couple of questions for me and then I'll decide the punishment for you."

"Help!" Jeffrey yelled. "Someone help me!"

Save your breath for answering my questions," Anánzu said acidly. "Now, true or false, you guys were the ones who destroyed the Iberian village."

"T… true," Jeffrey stammered. "We… the evil Riders impersonated Iberian guards with orders to kill and destroy everybody and everything!"

"Now we're getting somewhere. Okay, next question: who orchestrated this little scheme?"

"I don't know." Anánzu added her arm to the dagger against his neck. "I'm serious," Jeffrey gagged. "I receive orders from Zachariah I don't know where he gets these ideas."

"Somehow I believe you." She lifted the dagger but kept her arm on his neck. "Your treachery wasn't as bad as Zachariah's but it still deserves retribution." She took the dagger and thrust it into the center of Jeffrey's trousers. Jeffrey let out the most anguished scream that Anánzu had ever heard. Without missing a beat, she removed the dagger, twirled it so that the blade was pointing down and jammed it up to the hilt through Jeffrey's arm and the table.

"Keep the dagger," Ananzu said as she turned to leave. "Think of it as a memento of our time together." Jeffrey was still crying tears of pain as she left the tent. Outside, her own Riders had gathered the twenty or so members of the evil Riders who had remained behind and herded them up to the tent where they could hear what happened to Jeffrey. Anánzu took out another dagger. "Now does anyone want to join him?" The twenty or so men just shook their heads. "That's what I thought now you're all going to tell us what you know about the attack on the Iberian village. And if I catch any of you lying, you'll end up like him." He gestured to the tent where bawling could be heard.

"Fear is a powerful motivator," Harold agreed sipping his tea.

"Not to mention torture," Captain Garan added.

Anánzu continued, "We found out that Gerard wasn't picked randomly. The organizer of this heinous plan chose that particular village because it was isolated, very little chance for aide to get to Gerard before their work was completed."

Ada came over and sat down beside them. "By organizer, do you mean that guy who kidnapped and tortured me?"

"He is Zachariah." She said the name with a shiver of disgust. "And while he is the leader of the evil Riders, he didn't plan the destruction of Gerard, just carried it out."

"Then who did?" Andros demanded to know.

"Unfortunately, even I couldn't get that information out. But we did find out that it's someone with a lot of magic, enough magic to command and receive respect from hundreds of soldiers and enough influence to organize a daring plan such as this. My guess is that it was someone in a high up position like a nobleman or a Sage."

"Are you saying a Sage orchestrated the destruction of Gerard?" Maran asked recalling Sage Mattonda's conversation in the woods a few nights before.

"I'm not saying anything for certain, but that is the logical conclusion."

"Is Daniel okay?" Maran asked Ada noticing the Princess's worried face.

"He's fine; one of Anánzu's healers is fixing his shoulder right now. But..."

"What is it?"

"It's Captain Vostock. I... feel sorry for him, tying him up like that." She cast one eye at the Morbian Captain who was tied to a tree with metal bonds, yelling every expletive at the Iberians and Riders of Tch'Kar that he could think of.

"Yes, but it was a necessary evil. He would've not stopped until everybody except you were killed," Anánzu pointed out.

"Anánzu, may I see you for a moment in private?" Marta asked.

"Of course you may, meina Utar." The two walked along the beach between the threshold of the brightness of the fire and the darkness of the night.

"Anánzu, at the terrorist Riders' fortress, before we parted, you said 'irndo win vi, meina Utar.'"

"It means go with victory, my..."

"Yes, I know what it means, but what I want to know is why you called me 'little Legendary?'"

Anánzu sighed, she had a feeling this question would come up. "Marta, look at my eye." She lifted her bangs out of her right eye. Marta gasped. Her hidden eye wasn't an eye at all, but a glowing swirl inside a socket.

"By the Guardians, what..."

"My family is descended from the original Legendaries. That's why my father tried to unite the twelve kingdoms of Tel-ána. It was in his blood. Anyway, a journal created by my ancestors said that one day, new Legendaries will arise and free Tel-ána from eternal darkness."

"You think that's me? How can you tell?"

"My eye isn't like this because the Guardians are punishing me, Marta," Anánzu explained letting the hair fall over her eye again. "But because the eye is a detector. In addition to my birth magic, my ability to enchant arrows and weapons, my eye has the ability to detect who is destined to carry on the work of the Legendaries. When I saw you fight the evil Riders, Marta, my eye saw a glow coming from you. You are the one, Marta, you are the little Utar."

Marta gasped. She fell down onto the cool sand. "I... I don't believe it. When I first started this, my only mission was to kill King Gladirus, whom I expected was behind the destruction of Gerard, but... now I feel like there's something much bigger at stake."

"Yes, Marta, you have a destiny. A great one, if my eye is to be believed."

"Anánzu... I'm only a child. I'm not supposed to come of age for four more years. I'm too young to have a destiny. Please, find someone else to save Tel-ána from eternal darkness."

Anánzu laid a hand on the child's shoulder. "Marta, I do not know when your destiny will reach out to you. Only the Guardians know that. But I promise you that when that time comes, I will aide you in whatever way I can."

Marta smiled for she had a feeling that Anánzu could be trusted. And she also knew that whenever or wherever her destiny chooses to present itself, that she wouldn't have to face it alone.

Sage Mattonda had arrived at a small canyon in Mishanko. The map that he found in the Morbian Guardian Journal showed that a canyon shaped like a wolf was the resting place for Geddon, the weapon of the Guardians.

If the text of the Guardian Journal was to be believed, then the Guardians did not fight their battles with just physical combat and magic, but with weapons that could move on their own. Large weapons, weapons that were over five times the size and width of a wagon and could move either on their own will or controlled by the Guardians. However, during that time, the Guardians used primarily raw magic. So someone using raw magic could control it. It was dangerous, using raw magic could kill someone who isn't a Guardian, but Sage Mattonda was confident in his abilities.

Sage Mattonda teleported down to the center of the canyon and began drawing a pattern in the dirt. The symbol, three circles, one within another, representing the Guardians' Dimension (the outer most circle), the sky (the middle circle), and Tel-ána (the inner circle) and four lines representing the universal directions, was the ancient logo of the Guardians. This logo has been whispered in the Council of Sages and never reproduced for fear of the Guardians raining a curse down on them all. Sage Mattonda placed his staff at the center of the logo and then retreated outside it. He tore a page from the copy of the Guardian Journal he made and began reading from it.

"Ancient magic from days gone by, come to my staff as I make my cry!" The logo glowed briefly before energy began gathering to the crystal on Sage Mattonda's staff. With each line of text that the Sage read, a portion of the symbol glowed. "Ancient weapon I summon thee, by the powers of the Guardians I set you free! I implore you to join me by my side so that together we may fight! Prepare to send my enemies to their end. Geddon, it's time for you to rise again!" The logo glowed brightly and a wall of light rose around the logo. Beams of light formed an outline of a strange object. Sage Mattonda made a triangle shape with his hands. "Rise, Geddon, arise!" Energy in the shape of a triangle penetrated the wall of light and began filling in the outline.

The thing that appeared was a large vehicle object with a thirty foot tower in the center. Metal bars extended from it like spokes on a wheel. Attached to the bars were different weapons. One was a miniature cannon barrel and another had a pair of claws on it. A third had a drill and a fourth had an axe blade. Red light came from various areas on it including a large jewel at the center of the tower part.

"It works, it works!" Sage Mattonda cried. He levitated his staff to his hand and pointed in a direction. "Go, Geddon, reveal your mighty power to all!" Geddon was surrounded in a glowing field and flew off. "Perfect, now all I need to do is contact the Council. But first..." The Sage aimed his staff on the ground and fired a burst of energy destroying the ancient Guardian logo. "The evidence must be destroyed." Sage Mattonda suddenly gasped and dropped to one knee. Using the raw magic in combination with his Sage magic was draining on Mattonda. He decided to contact the Council later. A little rest won't flaw up his plans.

The next morning, the Iberians, the Morbians, Anánzu, and her Riders of Tch'Kar got ready to leave.

"The best way to contact the Council of Sages is to contact a Sage," Harold reminded them. "And once this comes around, I do not think the Kashuto Sage will help you."

"Captain Garan, I think we should return to Morbia," Ada suggested. "Sage Petro will gladly assist us."

"Perfect," Captain Vostock said. It was the first time he has said anything in a while. "Now you all can be judge for your crimes under His Highness, King Adleton!"

"Oh be quiet," Andros said jabbing him in the head.

"Chief Anánzu, Chief Anánzu," one of Anánzu's Riders of Tch'Kar called out. "Somebody's coming!" Everybody turned to get their weapons ready. An outline of a figure carrying a staff appeared. "It's a Sage!"

But as the figure appeared, everybody realized that it wasn't Sage Mattonda or Sage Petro. His robes were more decorated than a normal Sage. He wore no headdress and his staff was a mixture of gold and silver.

"It's High-Sage Laermos!" One of Vostock's followers realized. Laermos was the overseer of the Council of Sages and as such, was not the Sage of any one kingdom. He was chosen through a democratic vote just like his predecessors were ever since the Council was first formed. To be visited by him was considered just as much an honor as any king, maybe even more so. Everyone genuflected.

"Arise," High-Sage Laermos commanded. "Such formalities do not interest me."

"Well, this has certainly been an exciting couple of days," Harold commented.

"Sage Petro of Morbia and Sage Ben-Salaam of Iberia contacted me and informed me of the situation," Laermos explained. "This has evolved to so much more than unexplained village genocide." He turned to Marta, Daniel, Andros, Maran, Ada, and Captain Garan. "If you all would come with me, please."

"We're actually going to the Council of Sages," Daniel said excited.

Marta turned to Anánzu. "Anánzu, I would like to request that you come with us. Your knowledge would be a big help in finally solving this mystery." She quickly turned to High-Sage Laermos. "With your permission, High-Sage."

High-Sage Laermos agreed, "This affects everyone here."

Anánzu smiled. "Of course, meina Utar. It would be an honor." High-Sage Laermos' eyes shifted to the right at Anánzu's pet name but other than that showed no visible reaction. Anánzu turned towards Captain Vostock. "And you're coming with us. You need to know the truth. Maybe it will put a little humility into that swollen head of yours." Captain Vostock grunted in return.

"Are you sure your Riders of Tch'Kar will be all right?" Captain Garan asked Anánzu.

"They will survive. They were able to capture and impersonate several Morbian guards after all."

"Then let us go." High-Sage Laermos waved his staff and a portal appeared. Marta and Daniel entered first followed by Ada and Andros. Maran floated in with Captain Garan behind him. Anánzu pushed Captain Vostock into the portal before going in herself. High-Sage Laermos was last, closing the portal behind him.

The evil Riders of Tch'Kar stormed the village of Boricina, on the South-East boarder of Iberia. The village had little, if any, defenses. Within no time, the men had been slain, and the women and children had been enslaved for the Riders' "personal use." No sooner had the evil Riders begun their return trip then they came across a platoon of Iberian soldiers. There was a heavy battle and in the chaos, the women and children were able to escape to a neighboring village. This was the scene that played all over Iberia. Some villages closed their gates to everyone, friend and foe alike. The Iberian forces, despite all their efforts, were stretched pretty thin and could not answer the distress summons coming in from all over the kingdom. The soldiers joining the rebellion against King Gladirus certainly didn't help the situation.

One village that was able to escape their massacre was Icthior, the tree village. When word reached Chief Bishcott that villages were being randomly attacked, he ordered the village to ascend into the treetops. Using the same rope and pulley system that some villages use to operate their gates, the houses and structures of the village were hidden by the thick tree foliage. So when the evil Riders of Tch'Kar breached the outer walls, they found nothing. Confused, they moved on.

When the Oracle announced that they had moved on, Chief Bishcott breathed a sigh of relief. "Iberia is in a period of unrest," he said.

"I agree," the Oracle replied stroking the boy Lad's head. "I sense that it has something to do with the King and the village that those two children came from."

Chief Bishcott nodded. He prayed to the Guardians that the children Marta and Daniel would be all right.

King Gladirus climbed out of a hollow stump that marked the exit point to the emergency escape passage from the throne room. He looked around the forest. It was quiet, too quiet.

The rustle of leaves came from behind him. King Gladirus pivoted his upper body to the side and held out his elbow just in time to catch an assaulting bandit in the solar plexus. The bandit staggered back and King Gladirus went on the offensive pinning the pudgy bald man up against a tree.

"I would rather die than become your slave," the man declared.

King Gladirus let out a sigh, "Is this what rumors are spreading about me? How sad. I have no desire to make you my slave but your cloak will suffice." King Gladirus stripped the man of his cloak and donned it himself. The cloak, however, was very baggy and King Gladirus was forced to cut strips from the bottom and used them to bind the man's feet and hands behind his back. As soon as the cloak was short enough that King Gladirus could walk without tripping over himself, he took the man's dagger. "I apologize for this," he said to the bandit. "But I must find some way to calm the uproar in Iberia before chaos truly erupts." He took off leaving the bandit tied up in the forest.

There was only one problem: King Gladirus had no idea where he was. Keeping the hood over his crown and his hands together in their sleeves like a monk to hide the ring, he decided to find the nearest village and ask directions to the Iberian capital.

Suddenly a foul stench came across his nose. King Gladirus had to back away before he became sick. "Guardians protect me, what is that odor?" He gagged. He looked ahead and saw the outer wall of a village. The doors looked like they exploded. King Gladirus recognized the stench as the aroma of decaying carcass, human carcass. Even though he felt like gagging, he went into the village. Most of the houses were nothing more than rubble. King Gladirus stepped on something metallic. It was a gold and silver dragon crest, the crest of one of his knights. "No, this can't be, this must've been the village those children came from. My God, had I known such atrocities would've taken place, I never..." A stick cracked behind him. For a moment, King Gladirus was glad that this village wasn't all death and destruction but his joy soon grew into caution as he recalled that most of the kingdom was out to get him. He readied the bandit's dagger. "Stand back," he warned the moving shadow. "Just because I'm an old man doesn't mean I know how to fight."

It is said that between Tel-ána and the Guardians' Dimension where deceased souls go is a pocket dimension. Souls that have departed go here to be judged whether or not they were worthy to enter the Guardians Dimension or if they're forced to roam Tel-ána in eternal pain forever. It is also here where the Sages held their council meetings. There were no walls, at least not in the sense that common folk know of. There was, however, a round table with thirteen chairs. On twelve chairs, as well as on the table itself, were symbols of the kingdom that

HAROLD RAY

each Sage represented. Although kingdoms are allowed to employ up to three Sages if they so wish, only one was chosen to represent that kingdom at the Council of Sages and most of the time it was the most senior Sage. The thirteenth chair was reserved for the High Sage who oversaw the council meetings and was thus exempt from representing any one kingdom.

The Iberians, along with Princess Adora, Anánzu, and Captain Vostock were in awe. People have whispered descriptions of the Council of Sages' meeting chamber but seeing it in person was beyond description. What's even more, they were invited there by High-Sage Laermos, who oversaw all meetings of the Council of Sages.

"Sage Petro contacted me shortly after you left Morbia," High-Sage Laermos explained appearing behind them. "We believe that the destruction of the Iberian village of Gerard is related to a much larger threat that all of Tel-ána is facing."

"I hate it when I'm right," Daniel said. The others looked at him oddly. "I had a feeling that there was something bigger here," he explained.

"Yes, and as soon as the others get here, we can discuss it," High-Sage Laermos said.

"What others?" No sooner had Captain Garan asked that when more Sages began pouring in through various portals. Everyone was nervous that they were actually witnessing an event few mortals have, a meeting of Sages. Soon, all the seats except three were filled and they were the seats belonging to the Morbian and Iberian Sages and High-Sage Laermos who quickly remedied that by sliding his staff into a holster on the side of the high-back chair and sat in it.

"We are all here, Sage Petro," High-Sage Laermos called. The center of the table glowed and an image of Sage Petro appeared. The image was omni directional meaning that no matter where you sat, it was like he was talking specifically to you. "Please go ahead."

"High-Sage," Sage Petro greeted. "I used a residual spell and discovered that someone has been using raw magic on our Guardian Journal." That caused a group gasp from the non-Sages in the room. Using any type of magic with the exception of protection magic on a Guardian Journal alone was a violation of every law of Tel-ána. So using raw magic, which had been outlawed ever since the days of the Guardians due to its destructive potential, on a Guardian Journal was considered blasphemy. Even some of the elder Sages in the room were aghast at it although they were more composed about expressing it.

"Sage Petro, did the residual spell reveal how long it has been since the raw magic had been used?"

"Yes, High-Sage, it wasn't too long, three days give or take. I'm afraid it's been open. I thought that I should check with the Council of Sages to decide whether or not I should open it to check."

"I understand, Sage Petro, please stand by." High-Sage Laermos turned towards the other Sages. "Fellow Sages, we face an event unprecedented since the Guardians bestowed upon us their gifts at the Time of Beginnings. At the risk of defying them, we must open a Guardian Journal to determine whether or not its magic had been used. I ask that the Council give approval to Sage Petro to remove the Guardian Journal from its resting place and bring it here. What say you?"

"Aye," the Sages said as one.

"Excuse me," Andros called. "But what does all this have to do with us?"

"Be quiet, thief, and show the Council some respect," Captain Garan snapped swatting the boy in the back of the head.

"We have reason to believe that the magic of a Guardian Journal has been released upon the will of Sage Mattonda Giersi," High-Sage Laermos explained. "Tell me, has he left inexplicably for the past week."

"We've only met Sage Mattonda a week ago," Marta said. "He was hostile towards Daniel, Andros, Maran, and me when we infiltrated the castle but helped us out a lot up until yesterday when he left. He told us that he was going to help protect King Gladirus from whoever has been trying to kill him."

"We have been suspicious of Sage Mattonda for quite some time," Sage Kimo of Costal Glen informed them. "He has been traveling to and from other kingdoms under pretense of various missions for King Gladirus but no formal announcement has been given to the Council. Unfortunately, the violation of the Morbian Guardian Journal gives evidence to our suspicions."

"Sage Petro, you have the permission of the Council of Sages to remove the Guardian Journal from its resting place and bring it here to the Council."

"As you command, High-Sage," Sage Petro said before the transmission ended.

"This is unprecedented," Captain Garan commented. "Never before has a Guardian Journal been open in front of a large group of people. Such an action is taboo!"

"Unfortunately, Captain Garan, Sage Mattonda has already violated the Guardian Journal by infusing it with raw magic," High-Sage Laermos said. "Compared to that, what we are about to do is considered a blessing."

The center of the table started to glow again as Sage Ben-Salaam, the junior Iberian Sage, appeared. "Please forgive my intrusion, High-Sage, but I can not get in touch with Sage Mattonda. He's not even answering the high-level summoning spell you gave me. And the rebellion in Iberia is heating up. I can not stop this without him."

"I thought as much. Do not worry, Sage Ben-Salaam, just do the best you can. I promise that your helpfulness in this crisis will not go unrewarded."

"It is an honor to serve the council." And Ben-Salaam's image disappeared.

"This only accentuates Sage Mattonda's guilt," Sage Vima of Pasornin, the only female Sage, said. "No reasonable Sage would dare ignore a high summons. We must find him and bring him into our custody!"

"Let us wait for the Guardian Journal to arrive first. We can not find him anyway so we must wait." When High-Sage Laermos made a decision, it was treated as if the decision was made by the Guardians themselves.

Sage Petro appeared carrying a Journal on a red throw pillow. He approached the table and placed the book in front of High-Sage Laermos. "High-Sage Laermos, my fellow Sages, I present to you the Guardian Journal of Morbia." He then sat at his place.

High-Sage Laermos nodded his approval then raised his arms up. The other Sages laid their hands on the crest of the kingdom that they represented. "Almighty Guardians, you who at the Time of Beginning infused us with your power, we humbly ask for forgiveness for what we are about to do!"

"May the Guardians' blessing shine down upon us," the other Sages recited. High-Sage Laermos wiped his hands on his cloak and then turned the cover of the Guardian Journal. The pages, which were at first blank, suddenly began spouting ancient words, ancient words that only the Sages could read. High-Sage Laermos quickly turned the pages. He stopped at the middle of the book and turned to Sage Petros. "Is this where you sensed it?"

"It is, High-Sage, towards the middle of the book."

High-Sage Laermos took his own staff and waved it over the Guardian Journal. The jaded orb set into its top glow a variety of other colors. "I was afraid of this. Sage Mattonda must have performed an illegal duplication spell on the journal and..."

"High-Sage," Andros called. "If Sage Mattonda had tampered with this journal, maybe he tampered with his own as well."

That caused a surprised reaction from the council. Andros couldn't believe that they never considered the fact that a Sage would open his own Guardian Journal. Opening one Guardian Journal was bad enough, but to open two, even a saint would condemn such an act. The Council of Sages discussed the possibility amongst their selves before High-Sage Laermos pounded his staff on the "floor" and resumed the meeting.

"If it is true that Sage Mattonda has looked in these journals specifically, then it can only mean one thing: Sage Mattonda is trying to awaken the Geddon."

"What?"

"That's impossible!"

"Is he trying to destroy us all?" The other Sages were outraged at the revelation.

"Excuse me, but what's a Geddon?" Maran asked. He received a suspicious and bewildered look from mostly everyone.

"Please forgive him," Marta said. "He has been stuck in a temple for as long as he could remember and has no memory of his own past."

High-Sage Laermos nodded. "That is the case with most that have passed on. In the Iberian Guardian Journal, there is a scripture which reads 'Ertsi Surinam al gidara ni whok du Tel-ana. Nein recardo et eluti. Modamo Sage eluti Geddon. Nein superna ro tih de nam can olbiva. Solo acconta de Gardan ni Morbia sah et know.'"

"What does that mean?" Ada asked.

"It means this: 'There exist the most powerful weapon in the world of Tel-ána. Nobody can recall the name. Modern Sages have titled it 'Geddon.' Neither magic nor physical attacks can destroy it. Only the Morbian Guardian Journal has knowledge to summon it.'"

"But why would Sage Mattonda awake this Geddon?" Ada asked. "He can't control it, can he?"

"Through raw magic, he can," High-Sage Laermos said.

The strange machine called Geddon plowed through the forest heading for the main doors that lead into Iberia. The guards at the gate quickly utilized their combined magic to shut the gates and board it tight. But it was no use, Geddon plowed through it like it wasn't even there.

Sage Mattonda watched the destruction from a distance as he continued to give it commands vie raw magic. Everything was going according to plan. Now was the time to contact the Council of Sages and "apprise" them of the situation.

"I am not sure why Sage Mattonda would want to awake Geddon," High-Sage Laermos said. "But if somebody doesn't stop it, it will destroy all of Tel-ána!"

"I wonder if it has something to do with the evil Riders of Tch'Kar," Maran thought out loud. Once again, everybody gave him an odd look.

"What did you say?" Andros asked fiercely.

"Well… after we escaped from the evil Riders' fortress, I saw Sage Mattonda go into the woods. I followed him and I saw him talking to one of the evil Riders so I wondered if…"

"And you didn't tell anyone?" Andros interrupted. He let out a sound of frustration. "I don't care if you're dead or not, I can't believe someone can be so stupid?"

"I didn't want to raise any concern if I turned out to be wrong."

"You mean you didn't say anything simply because you were afraid that YOU WERE WRONG?" Andros asked, his tone getting louder with each word. "I wish you were solid so I could knock some sense into that brainless head of yours." The ghost cowered from the thief.

"Maran, it's all right," Marta assured him. She went to put a hand on his shoulder but ended up going right through him again. "You didn't know. And besides, Sage Mattonda fooled us…" Her pink eyes widened. She turned to Anánzu and asked hurriedly, "Anánzu, you said that the evil Riders were responsible for Gerard's destruction."

"Yes, I got the confession directly from the mouth of my former advisor."

"And you also said that it was someone with a lot of magic?"

"Yes."

Marta turned to Maran, "Maran, you said that you saw Sage Mattonda talking to the evil Riders?"

"It sounded like he was giving them orders," Maran commented. Marta's already pale face got as white as Maran. She dropped to her knees.

High-Sage Laermos' staff glowed. He nodded to Sage Petro who stood by Marta and her friends and placed a shield around them so they would appear invisible to everyone in the room and whoever was trying to contact them. And if High-Sage Laermos' suspicions about the sender's identity were true, then they had to keep up the illusion of naiveté.

"Now what's going on?" Captain Vostock wondered. Sage Petro hushed him.

The combined crests on the table started to glow. Sage Mattonda appeared on the center of the table. "My fellow Sages, I bring terrible news. An ancient weapon of the Guardians had been awakened by King Gladirus. Geddon is an ancient machine that the Guardians used in their battles against the Forces of Darkness. I consulted some archivists and they all confirmed the information. It has already breached the gates of Iberia and is now heading for Ricardo Castle. I will try to stop it to the best of my abilities."

"Do not, Sage Mattonda," High-Sage Laermos instructed. "Try to save as many lives as you can. We shall organize a counter-strategy."

"Understood, High-Sage." Sage Mattonda's image disappeared as well as the invisible shield surrounding Marta and the others.

"King Gladirus' magic is not strong enough to summon something like the Geddon," High-Sage Laermos pointed out. "Only the magic of a Sage can awaken and control such a threat."

"Sage... Sage Mattonda ordered my village to be destroyed!" Marta's words were barely a whisper. "I... I trusted him and..."

"I hate to say I told you so," Andros said. "but I did warn you. And it hurts, doesn't it? It hurts a lot to be betrayed by your own people."

"Shut your mouth, Thief," Captain Garan snapped grabbing Andros by the collar of his shirt. "Do you have any idea what it's like to be betrayed on such a scale?"

"You'd be surprised," Andros muttered darkly.

"Marta's sadness is understandable," High-Sage Laermos said. "However, seeking vengeance is not a luxury we can afford right now. Only the Guardians can control and neutralize weapons like the Geddon. Unfortunately, they have long since transcended Tel-ána and there is nobody alive with the same power or skill as the Guardians. I'm afraid that it is up to all of you. You must destroy it or else it will eventually escape from Sage Mattonda's control and run amuck through all of Tel-ána."

"And why do you want us to do it?" Andros asked. "You're the Council of Sages; your power comes directly from the Guardians. So why do you want us to sacrifice ourselves?"

"It's the prophecy," Marta mumbled. She looked up at Anánzu who nodded. "We are the Utars; the Legendaries, it's our destiny to deliver Tel-ána from eternal darkness. If Geddon succeeds in devastating all of Tel-ána, then we will be in eternal darkness."

"Marta is correct," High-Sage Laermos threw in. "My elder once told me that the Legendaries are blessed directly by the Guardians rather than by Sages, so only the Legendaries would stand any chance. But it will be a very difficult battle. Therefore, I am giving each of you the option of participating in this battle or not. Please keep in mind that backing out is not an act of cowardice and you will all be treated the same with either choice you will make. So what say you, will you go or will you not go?"

"I must participate in it," Marta said with a firmness that made her sound older than she actually was. She stood straight up and stepped forward.

"And I shall be by your side, meina Utar," Anánzu said stepping up beside her.

"It is my sworn duty to protect Iberia and its king. I will go." Captain Garan raised his sword in a knight's vow.

"I will go too," Daniel said. "Marta's my only living relative. I'm not leaving her."

"I will also go," Ada said.

"But Princess Adora!" Captain Vostock protested.

"Captain, I will not hear your segregated views on the Iberians now, of all times!" Ada snapped. Vostock's eyes bugged out (an amused look to Captain Garan), the Princess had never used such a harsh tone against him before. "Geddon is a threat to all of Tel-ána, including Morbia. We must stop it before it harms anyone else."

Captain Vostock sighed and stepped up beside the Princess. "Then I, as Captain of the Morbian Guard, shall protect you with my life." Captain Garan raised an eyebrow. Vostock gave him a piercing stare. "I have no feelings for Iberians, I will shed no tears if they die or not. But my Princess insists on participating in this foolhardy action and I must protect her."

"Since Marta's going, I will have to go too," Maran chimed in.

Everybody turned to look at Andros. He was the only one who hadn't stepped forward. Everybody could tell that he wasn't willing to go through this. He was reluctant from the beginning, only getting involved because Marta and Daniel forced him to. Then, to everyone's surprise, Andros did step forward. He offered no reason for stepping up and nobody asked him for it.

High-Sage Laermos summoned a portal and everybody found themselves back in Kashuto at Harold's Lighthouse. Anánzu's Riders of Tch'Kar and Vostock's elite guard were still there.

"Prepare to move out," Anánzu instructed. "We have to aid the Utars even if it costs us our lives. The Riders of Tch'Kar are about to fulfill their original objective."

"Ma'am," they saluted.

"Mount up," Vostock ordered his own guards. "We are going to Iberia."

"Are we going to destroy it, Captain?" One guard asked. Captain Vostock just grumbled.

"I'll ask Uncle Harold to summon some horses for us," Ada volunteered. Harold did so and they all took off for Iberia. As the battalion of horses galloped through Barrel Pass towards the Kashuto-Morbia boarder, Marta looked around at the small force they gathered. Herself, Daniel, Ada, Captain Garan, Andros, and Maran along with Anánzu and her Riders of Tch'Kar and Captain Vostock and his elite guard. All together, there were about forty of them. But from what High-Sage Laermos told them about this Geddon weapon, it might not be enough. Plus even if by some miracle or gift of the Guardians they do manage to destroy Geddon, they will still have to deal with Sage Mattonda. Deep down, Marta wasn't sure they would be able to succeed. Well, at least when she dies, she'll be reunited with her family. Her father, in one of his extremely rare tranquil moments, told her once that for something to live, something else must die. But if something had to die, then something must live in return. That was known as the Law of the Guardians, kill in order to live. Marta wasn't exactly sure what it meant back then, but now she thought she did. She would die so others may live.

Sage Mattonda watched as Geddon tore through another Iberian village, leaving destruction and even death in its wake. He smiled. Soon, it will be time and then, Iberia and all of Tel-ána, will belong to him.

"Marta," Maran called. "Look ahead." The Iberians, Morbians, and Riders of Tch'Kar exited Barrel Pass on the Morbia side.

And froze in their tracks.

Looking down from a bluff, they saw row after row of scruffy, sinister-looking men. And they looked very familiar.

"It's the dark Riders of Tch'Kar," Anánzu confirmed. She gripped her horse's reigns. "The Guardians must've decided not to accept them as well."

"After what they've done, I am not surprised," one of the Riders of Tch'Kar said.

"Any ideas on how we're going to get passed them?" Captain Garan asked. "Going through them seems to be definitely out."

"How many do you think there are?" Vostock asked.

"3,000 at least," Andros called from on Ada, who had transformed into a gargoyle and was carrying Daniel and himself. "Too much to fight hand to hand."

"Even my arrows wouldn't be able to get all of them."

"Then we must sneak around them," Marta said. They descended the bluff on an angle from the evil Riders, who were already moving south. "Hey, are they going to attack the Morbian castle?"

"If they are, then they are going in the wrong direction," Captain Vostock pointed out. "The castle is to the east, not the south."

Marta gasped. "Then... that means they're heading for Iberia!"

"Then we must get there ahead of them and stop Geddon before they arrive," Captain Garan said. Unfortunately, they didn't get far before they were spotted.

"Squads 1-3 after them," sounded Zachariah's voice (a voice Anánzu knew only too well). "Destroy them! Everyone else, move forward."

Vostock, his guards, Captain Garan, and Anánzu's Riders of Tch'Kar moved into battle. They fought hard but the evil Riders also put up a good fight. The evil Riders were ruthless and without magic proof armor, some of Anánzu's weaker Riders immediately fell. Marta, Anánzu, Maran, Andros, Ada, and Daniel moved away and tried to move ahead of the main force but Zachariah and a squadron of extremely muscular armor-clad guards blocked their way.

"So we meet again, my little Dove," Zachariah said licking his lips.

Anánzu cocked a bow with one of her silver arrows. "Zachariah, today's the day you will pay for all your crimes."

"By crimes, do you mean kidnapping Princess Adora? Or was it betraying you to the enemy? Or maybe..." Marta didn't think that Zachariah's smirk could get any more sinister, but somehow it did. "It was what I did to your daughter?"

"You have no right to speak of her," Anánzu hissed.

"I see; you're still haunted about what I did to her while you weren't looking. All I can say is... it was a rather enjoyable experience... for me anyway."

Anánzu let out a scream of rage and was about to fire her arrow when one of Zachariah's guards came up behind her and knocked her to the ground. Andros seized this opportunity to drop from Ada's back and landed on the back of Zachariah's horse. He held a dagger to the leader's neck.

"Back off from them or I'll slit your throat," he threatened.

Zachariah just laughed. His body was charged with lightning and the shock threw Andros off.

"Oh no!" Daniel gasped.

"Hold on, Daniel," Ada said using her massive wings to get herself airborne.

"Where are we going?" Daniel asked.

"To get help."

Upon seeing Zachariah's surprise attack on Andros, Anánzu gasped. She knew Zachariah's magic was to create balls of lava. The only way one could obtain more than one magic is if they were taught by a Sage. But Anánzu wasn't just surprised about that. She figured that Sage Mattonda would teach him something like that even though stealing someone's magic was considered cannibalistic, even if a Sage was to do it. What she was surprised at was the alternate magic he decided to use, charging one's own body with lightning. She knew of only one other person with such a magic: her daughter, Aleeta. That's what he meant when he said 'what I did to her while you weren't looking.' She came to the horrible and sickening conclusion that Zachariah didn't just kill her, but he drained her magic, her very soul.

She snapped. "You... MONSTER!" Swinging her longbow like a melee weapon, she lunged at Zachariah. The leader of the evil Riders chuckled as he blocked all of Anánzu's strikes with his sword while counterattacking with bursts of lightning.

"That's right, this was the magic wielded by your daughter Aleeta," Zachariah said. "I violated her body and soul, I took her magic; she can't even cross over to the Guardian Dimension and rest in peace! And it's all thanks to the Arcadia spell, a little gift from Sage Mattonda." Zachariah burst into laughter.

"Arcadia spell?" Andros questioned getting up. "Now I'm mad!" Brandishing both of his daggers he charged Zachariah from behind. Once again, Zachariah charged his body with lightning and threw both Andros and Ananzu off. Even though he was still taking the effects of Zachariah's lightning attack Andros thrusted his daggers trying to penetrate Zachariah. "Compared to some of the punishment I've received, this is nothing."

"Then you won't mind if I turn it up a notch." The lightning started to spread. Andros couldn't hold on and was thrown back. He fell to the ground smoking.

"Andros!" Marta cried out. She extended her quarterstaff and leaped from her horse. In mid-air, she jabbed her staff with all her strength. She got Zachariah in the shoulder and knocked him off his own horse. Both of them crashed to the ground but Marta was the first to stand. She aimed her staff at Zachariah as if daring him to make a move. "Andros, get away quickly!"

"Right," Andros said getting up and hobbling away. "Thanks."

Anánzu was still stunned from the lightning attack. "Aleeta... had too much control to allow her magic to run wild like that."

Zachariah looked up and although it was Marta standing before him, it wasn't Marta that he saw, but a girl with purple hair that came down to her earlobes in a bowl-shape. Her eyes weren't pink, but green.

"A... Aleeta!" Zachariah cried. His eyes had a look of fear in them. "It... it can't be, you're dead! I killed you! I KILLED YOU!" Zachariah was unable to stop the memories from coming forth, and the pain associated with them.

Six years ago, the Iberian Sage named Mattonda Giersi came to him with an offer that was just too good to be true. If he and the other Riders of Tch'Kar would start causing chaos throughout Iberia, the Sage would guarantee them, and especially Zachariah, a high position in the new Iberian government.

Zachariah immediately agreed.

But first he needed to get rid of the current leadership, meaning Anánzu and her family. Only then would he have unchallenged reign to move the Riders of Tch'Kar in a new direction, a more prosperous direction.

That night, a team of Iberians loyal to Sage Mattonda invaded the camp. Zachariah recruited some others and killed all the guards allowing them to loot and plunder as they wish. Zachariah himself agreed to take care of the leadership: Anánzu, her father, and her daughter Aleeta. He invaded the tent but couldn't find Anánzu or her father. However, someone was waiting for him, Aleeta. Aleeta had a feeling that Zachariah would turn out to be a traitor and stayed behind to put a stop to him once and for all. Aleeta and Zachariah unleashed their full magic on each other.

The battle was intense, destroying the encampment and even some of the Iberian soldiers in the process. Trained by her mother and Grandfather, Aleeta, despite her young age, put up a fight that, had anyone but him knew about it, would sing it until the Guardians returned. But in the end, through some rather underhanded techniques, Zachariah emerged triumphant. He then decided to help himself to her magic using the spell that Sage Mattonda taught him as a gesture of good faith to their alliance. He stripped off her clothing and clutched her close to him. He began chanting the incantation, ripping into her very soul, where it is said that the very source of all of Tel-ána's magic lies. The girl struggled with all her might but eventually succumbed to the spell. Little magical bursts exited from Aleeta's body and into Zachariah's. Creating little spikes on his fingers, he did the final, gruesome act of the spell, using the spikes to stab into her skin and soak up some of her blood. The draining completed, Zachariah dropped her lifeless body to the ground, for in draining the magic from her soul; he drained her very life force in the process and she didn't have enough to survive even if a healer were to get to her in time. He stood and licked the blood from his fingers. Her magic, her very soul, belonged to him.

Suddenly his body started to convulse. A phantom image of Aleeta appeared before him. Zachariah screamed, for he was afraid he had invoked the wraith of the Guardians and they were sending her to him as a punishment. When he blinked, she was gone and Zachariah decided that it was just an aftereffect of the draining and dismissed it.

What Sage Mattonda (unintentionally) failed to tell him was that the draining of a person's magic isn't supposed to last as long as Zachariah did with Aleeta. The draining was only supposed to be brief, because excessive draining could kill the person being drained and the excessive and continuous draining of magic causes hallucinations to appear in the mind of the drainer. Obviously, Zachariah did not know this.

When Anánzu and her father returned to search for Aleeta, they discovered her nude and lifeless corpse tied to a tree. Anánzu screamed for what seemed like days. Zachariah, his followers, and the Iberians who originally attacked them were nowhere to be seen.

Zachariah still continued to suffer hallucinations due to the draining of Aleeta's magic. Eventually, he got used to them and was even able to drown them out. Since then, he has drained numerous opponents of their magic with the spell. It did not matter if they were young or old, male or female, if they had magic that he wanted, he would get it and since he never seemed to have any hallucinations of any of the other people whose magic he drained, he thought he was rid of the hallucinations until he was attacked by a girl who looked uncannily similar to Aleeta and the hallucinations attacked him full force!

"I see that I'm not the only one who's haunted by Aleeta's death," Anánzu commented as Captain Garan, blood-stained armor from going through an entire squad of evil Riders, killed one of Zachariah's guards and helped her up by draping an arm across both his shoulders. "I'm guessing Aleeta didn't make it easy for him so many years ago." Anánzu smiled. "He may have been able to kill her and absorb her magic, but she left an impact on him, a rather unsatisfactory impact, at least for him." Anánzu smiled. "Good girl, Aleeta, defiant even beyond the end."

"Why aren't you dead, why aren't you dead?" Zachariah was asking over and over again. Another of Zachariah's guards got Marta into a bear hug and began squeezing her. Marta screamed.

Zachariah's original smugness returned even through the hallucinations. "I don't know how you survived my draining but by the time the day is through, I'll be the only one going into Iberia!" Zachariah's voice had taken on an insane tone to him. This was another effect of his constant use of the magic draining technique: insanity.

Zachariah's laughing was drowned out by a horn playing a heroic charge-type song.

"That's the Morbian war song," Captain Vostock realized.

From the forest came row after row of knights, all bearing the eagle and starburst crest of King Adleton. Like a moving wall, they approached the evil Riders of Tch'Kar. The evil Riders utilized all their magic but it bounced off of their armor. The knights struck them down quickly and efficiently.

"No, it can't... this can't be happening!" Zachariah whined.

"But it is," came a deep voice. King Adleton appeared. He was decked out in gold armor with a gold helmet with crown decoration attachment and sitting upon a white horse also in armor. Ada and Daniel flanked him. The rest of Zachariah's guards moved in to attack King Adleton but Ada and Daniel utilized their magic and weapons to devastate them. King Adleton used his energy magic to disintegrate Zachariah's remaining guards then turned on Zachariah himself.

"You monster, what do you want?" Zachariah shouted.

"You're the real monster," King Adleton said. "You attacked that Iberian village and tried to blame it on us. You use forbidden magic with no regards or remorse for those you affected. You kidnapped, assaulted, and drained magic from my own daughter! I do not tolerate such dishonor!" He held out his hand and fired a gold sphere of energy. The gold sphere of energy hit Zachariah's body. Zachariah's rational mind had deteriorated because of the magic draining he performed on Aleeta and others. His scream was almost inhuman. He tried to summon his own magic, but he couldn't focus his mind enough to do it. King Adleton fired another energy sphere then several more. Collapsing to the ground, strange multi-color strands of energy began smoking from Zachariah's body.

"What's going on?" Daniel asked.

"I believe that all the magic he has drained over the years is being freed," Captain Garan said.

"And from the looks of it, he had drained a lot," King Adleton observed.

One of the last mists that emitted took the form of Aleeta. She smiled gently at her mother before disappearing.

"Guardians," Anánzu muttered. "Please help my daughter find eternal peace with you."

King Adleton fired a few more of his spheres of light and disintegrated Zachariah's body, leaving only a scorched imprint in the ground.

"Your Highness," Captain Vostock cried dropping to both knee. The others, not belonging to the Morbia, simply bowed out of respect. "Forgive me, Your Highness, I tried to bring your daughter back, but..."

"And you did," King Adleton interrupted. "She is back with me; perhaps she is now more wiser than me." King Adleton turned to

Marta and the others. "I was contacted by the Council of Sages. They informed me of what's happening. When my daughter and the Iberian boy appeared, I took a platoon ahead and reinforcements will not be far behind." He smiled at the group. "We will handle these vandals; you must deal with Mattonda and Geddon."

"Right," Marta agreed. She and the others got back on their horses and took off.

Daniel turned to King Adleton. "You should be proud of your daughter, Your Highness. She helped us a lot during our journey."

"I know, and that's why I'm not grounding her for life. But we'll have a long talk about going off without telling me directly later." Ada's face grew red.

Daniel looked like he wanted to say something else but didn't want to chance ending up like Zachariah. "Well... good luck, Your Highness." He turned to leave.

"Wait a moment, boy," King Adleton called. Daniel stopped. "To tell you the truth, I don't trust you Iberians to handle a task this big. And Iberian children to boot." Daniel's head lowered in embarrassment. King Adleton smiled. "So I've decided to send a representative to the battle." Daniel sensed that King Adleton planned on saying this. "And I am sending my daughter, Princess Adora, as that representative. She has my blood in her and that alone guarantees victory." Daniel's face lit up when King Adleton told him that Ada was coming along. "Despite not being from Morbia, I am assigning you the task of protecting her. Can you do that, boy?"

"I won't let you down, Your Highness," Daniel said.

"Just make sure you treat her with respect."

"Father, the problem isn't that he doesn't treat me with respect, it's that I don't treat him with enough respect." And before anyone could retort that, she transformed herself into a giant eagle and picked up Daniel in her talons. She flew off.

King Adleton watched them fly off and then scowled at the spot where Zachariah used to be. He fired a sphere of energy forming a small crater in the ground and then returned to the battle.

Sage Mattonda watched this drama play out. It seemed that Zachariah and his ruthless Riders of Tch'Kar were worthless when they were really needed.

He smiled. "Oh well, they don't matter any more. I have everything I need. I think it's time for the final conflict to commence." He disappeared.

Marta, Anánzu, Maran, Captains Garan and Vostock, and Andros arrived at the Iberian boarder with Morbia. The first thing they noticed was the smashed gate.

"Something tells me Geddon was here," Maran said.

"You think so?" Andros asked sarcastically.

"This won't be like blasting open the gates to the village," Marta commented. "It's just too big for me to handle alone."

"We'll need to clear all this rubble before we are to continue," Captain Garan said as Daniel and Ada joined them. Marta, Anánzu, and Andros utilized their magic to turn the pieces of the gate into rubble.

"This is taking too long," Captain Vostock said when they were doing this chore for about five minutes. "Geddon already has a head start from us."

"That's correct," Sage Mattonda said as he appeared in front of them. "And all of you are powerless to stop it."

"You selfish dog!" Captain Garan insulted. "I'll teach you for betraying our noble king."

"Your noble king is an old fossil who's just waiting to die," Mattonda said. "I shall bring new, better leadership to all of Tel-ána."

"Iberia shall never fall under the dictatorship of a boar like you!"

"Nor shall Morbia," Captain Vostock threw in. The two Captains drew their swords and charged Sage Mattonda. Sage Mattonda was able to fend them off with his staff then blasted them with a burst of energy. He then turned to Marta, Daniel and Andros. "I should have killed all of you when I had the chance. Now may be the last time for me to do it."

"You were the one who destroyed Gerard!" Marta accused.

"You finally got it right," Sage Mattonda said with a smirk. "Better late than never, I suppose. It was so easy manipulating all of you in to thinking Morbia was the culprit. Like helpless lambs, you allowed yourselves to be ushered around. In some way, it's kind of sad. But even though you finally know the truth, it is too late now to do anything about it."

"That's what you think!" Daniel said as he unleashed his talisman's full power at the rogue Sage.

"Allow me to show you what a Sage Talisman is really capable of." Sage Mattonda's own talisman released energy in a spiral formation that Daniel couldn't dodge. Sage Mattonda turned and struck Maran just as he was about to possess the Sage. The Sage demonstrated that his vast array of magic could affect even ghosts. And unlike Zachariah, he didn't need to drain it from anybody. Being a Sage entitled him to a wide arsenal of magical abilities. Sage Mattonda energized his staff and struck Anánzu with it, throwing her into Captain Vostock.

Marta took out her quarterstaff. She charged towards him but Sage Mattonda just lifted her up into the air telekinetically. "Face it, child, you'll never beat me."

"Marta!" Andros called out. He placed his hands on the ground and caused a humungous vine to sprout up under Sage Mattonda and wrapped him in its vice grip. The Sage lost his hold on Marta and she fell to the ground. Ada (transformed into a horse) and Daniel ran by and picked her up just before the Sage broke free.

"Bind!" Anánzu called out as she fired two of her arrows. The arrows turned into metal clamps which bound Sage Mattonda's arms and legs.

"It doesn't matter if you capture me or not," Sage Mattonda said. "You'll never stop Geddon, only I have the power. And soon, I'll have all the power." An explosion of energy broke Anánzu's bindings and Sage Mattonda stabbed his staff into the ground. Explosions came from underneath everyone and knocked them out.

All except Maran, who could only watch in horror as the others were knocked unconscious. He turned towards the Sage. "How could you? What right do you have to try to hurt them?"

"They attacked me; all I did was retaliated."

Deep down, Maran was afraid. It seemed like he had been afraid ever since Marta and Daniel found him. He then recalled the courage and bravery expressed by his new friends. The time for being scared was over, now was the time for action. Maran's fear was replaced by a new emotion, an emotion he hadn't felt before: fury. "Well I won't let you attack anyone ever again!" Maran's hands started to glow. As Maran got more and more angry, his hand glowed brighter and brighter.

Sage Mattonda was genuinely surprised. "What is this?"

Maran held out his hands. A blue spark of energy came out from them and struck the ground in front of Sage Mattonda. With a loud scream, the spark became a steady stream of blue energy which found its target in Sage Mattonda. Sage Mattonda tried setting up a force field but the unexpected attack pushed him back about fifty yards.

"That was ecto-projection," Sage Mattonda realized. "Only ghosts who... no, it couldn't be!" Sage Mattonda slammed his staff on the ground and disappeared.

Maran was scared at what he just did; he never experienced this type of magic before. Maran decided to ponder it later, seeing that the others were beginning to come around.

"What hit me?" Daniel asked.

"I'm sorry," Maran apologized. "I tried to stop him but I couldn't."

"You took on a Sage by yourself?" Andros questioned. "I don't know if that's either really brave or really stupid."

"Well I thought it was brave," Marta said.

"I don't know what happened," Maran said. "I just felt this emotion build up until... I blasted him."

"Just when I think I have you figured out, Maran, you surprise me again," Daniel commented.

"Sorry."

"Don't be, it probably saved all of us."

"You tried your best, Maran, that's all anybody expects," Ada comforted.

"Well as heartwarming as this is, we still have an ancient all-powerful weapon to stop," Andros reminded. "Or at least try to stop."

"He's right," Anánzu said. "We may not be able to stop it, but that doesn't mean we can't try." She turned to Ada. "Ada, transform into a dragon and carry us over the gate." Ada nodded and transformed. She tried to extend her size as much as possible. She managed to grow enough for Marta, Daniel, Andros, and Anánzu to hop on her back. Captain Garan and Vostock had to hold on to her talons.

"Marta," Andros called. "Thank you, it seems that I owe you."

"Let's just say we're even," Marta said smiling.

Geddon was rapidly approaching the Iberian capitol. The perimeter guards, who had been witness to the rebellion against King Gladirus (and had not taken any one side), now turned their attention to the approaching weapon, first pointed out to them by a windwaker. One guard gave out a signal to another and the second guard utilized his magic to open a large chasm in front of Geddon. Geddon stopped and seemed to be studying the chasm for a moment. Then a strange glowing force field surrounded it and it began levitating itself across the chasm.

"By the Guardians, what kind of monster is this?" One guard asked.

"Stand firm," the Captain ordered. "We can't let that thing get to the capitol!" The guards drew swords and charged Geddon. Geddon's drill started up and lanced out towards one of the guards.

It drilled through the guard's armor and his body like it was wood. As the guard's body fell to the ground, blood spilling out of all sides, the remaining guards were hesitant in continuing their attack. That hesitation was all Geddon needed to bypass the guards and continue on to the capitol.

The Iberians and their allies entered to find the capital in pure chaos. Conflicts between loyalists to King Gladirus and rebels had resulted in wanton destruction all over the place.

"This is horrible!" Ada gasped.

"I always expected the capitol to be like this," Captain Vostock commented drawing a dirty glance from Captain Garan. "But now that I see it in person, I can take no pleasure out of it."

Marta ran up to two people who were fighting. "Stop it!" She cried. "You two shouldn't be fighting!"

"Shut your mouth, girl," one snapped. "This heretic will die!"

"I won't let Iberia fall into tyranny under the dictatorship of King Gladirus," the other replied.

Marta quickly launched two vibro-shocks which knocked the combatants down. "Listen, you idiots, the only thing you're doing is helping the real villain here, Sage Mattonda."

One of the combatants got up and lifted Marta up by her neck. "How dare you talk about the Sage that way, you have no right calling yourself an Iberian." He was choking Marta so hard that she was afraid she was going to pass out.

Captain Garan slugged him so hard that he dropped Marta and fell to the ground unconscious.

"Captain Garan!" Ada gasped.

"As patriotic as I am," he said helping Marta up. "Even I can not stand by while a child is hurt. Life takes priority over all, even loyalty." He turned towards the other fighter, "There is a powerful weapon of destruction coming this way. If you know what's good for you, you will take your family as far away from here as possible.

It doesn't matter where you go, just as long as you don't stay in the capitol. You will know when it is safe to return."

"R... right," the man stammered and quickly took off.

"What is this, the Time of Beginning?" Andros asked. "Has everyone deteriorated into savages?"

"It would seem that way," Maran said solemnly.

"We need to get everyone out of here," Daniel said. "Let's split up and evacuate as many people as we can."

The group split up. Marta, Daniel, Maran, and Ada warned the people who were hiding in the houses while Captain Garan, Vostock, Andros, and Anánzu warned those who were outside. Anyone who tried to start a fight with them would only end up getting possessed by Maran or knocked out by the Captains. Soon, the capital was mostly deserted. Everyone met up again at the center plaza.

"Mostly everyone's escaped," Marta said. "What do we do now?"

"I'm afraid that's all we can do," Anánzu said solemnly. "Everyone who wanted to escape has and those who haven't will once they see Geddon."

"Help! Help me, please!" Everyone turned to see a man running through the streets being chased by a strange metal object.

"It's Geddon," Captain Vostock said.

"Here we go, the moment of truth," Garan said.

"That's Geddon?" Daniel asked. "It's enormous!"

"Yeah, and its armor looks impenetrable," Andros added.

"For all our sake, you better be wrong," Marta said.

"We must attack it now!" Captain Garan said drawing his sword.

"For once, I agree with you, Iberian," Captain Vostock agreed. The two drew their swords and charged Geddon. A mere ten feet from Geddon, a force field was raised and repelled them.

"It was ready for us," Captain Garan groaned.

"It can't stop what it can't see," Captain Vostock said using his invisibility magic. To increase his chances of success, he ran around to the side and attacked that way. But once again, he hit the force field instead. He became visible and Geddon attacked with its laser arm.

Captain Garan ran in between and deflected the blast to the best of his ability. "Magic may not be able to affect it, but it can still affect us!" The blast began pushing Captain Garan back.

Vostock couldn't believe that he was saved by an Iberian. To him, it was probably the ultimate humiliation. But he was a man of honor above anything else. He would not let Garan's attempt at heroism go unpaid. Vostock took his sword and sliced down on the energy beam. The beam was now hitting the sword instead.

"Vostock?"

"Move now," Vostock instructed. Garan twisted to the side just as the high-powered energy beam broke the sword. The blast barely missed Captain Garan.

"Thank you," Garan said.

"We are even," Vostock simply replied.

Geddon got past all of their defenses and proceeded into the town, crushing everything and everyone in its path. The group gave chase.

Marta was shocked at the terrible destructive power displayed by Geddon. What was Sage Mattonda thinking releasing such power?

"Marta," Daniel called. "Let's go, we have to destroy it!"

"I... I can't," Marta stuttered. "I need time to build up my magic." That was only half the truth. While Marta did need time to perform her dance, she was also scared, scared of challenging a weapon of such incredible size and power.

"Fine, we'll handle it then." The others moved forward. Daniel led the attack with his talisman with Anánzu backing him up with her arrow. The two attacks did nothing to harm it. Maran tried to phase through the shield to take control of Geddon but not even he could get through its impenetrable barrier. In fact, trying to get through the barrier was actually causing him pain if that was possible.

"It's just like what the Guardian Journal said," Andros said as he summoned a large vine to wrap around Geddon. "Neither magic nor weapons can stop it."

Marta was thinking Andros is right! There's nothing we can do about it! It's over, Tel-ána is doomed! She lowered her head in defeat.

"Are you giving up, Marta?" A voice asked startling Marta. Marta turned around as King Gladirus stepped out from behind a house. He lowered the hood on his cloak.

"King Gladirus! I'm sorry to be the one telling you this, Your Highness, I'm afraid the one who tricked you was Sage Mattonda."

"What?" King Gladirus asked shocked. "That can't be true, can it?"

Sadly, Marta nodded her head. "The Council of Sages will confirm it."

"So, that explains why he wasn't with me when the rebellion started."

"I'm sorry, Your Highness, we didn't find out until recently." Marta's head lowered in defeat and remorse.

King Gladirus paused before saying, "Marta, you never did answer my question. Are you giving up?"

Marta looked up at her king. "I... I don't want to but... I don't see how there's no other choice."

"Don't worry, Marta, everything will be all right. You won't know if you fail unless you just try. Trust me."

Despite herself, Marta laughed harshly. "I trusted Sage Mattonda, and he turned out to be the one who ordered my village to be destroyed."

"Well, what about your father?" King Gladirus asked. "Do you trust him?"

Marta gasped. How did King Gladirus know her father? Marta thought back and could vaguely recall her father regularly praising King Gladirus, saying he was a man of honor, always true to his word. Even though they constantly were at odds, Marta trusted her father more than she trusted anyone, even Daniel. If he trusted King Gladirus, then so could she.

Marta closed her eyes and began her dance. While she was developing her magic, her mentor instructed her to imagine music and let her movements flow with it. Every movement, every time a part of her body moved, she was gathering energy and if she hesitated for even a moment, she could lose the energy that she had gathered and would have to start over again. But that was not the case today. Her movements were like a rushing river, smooth in movement yet extremely strong. Everything slipped from her mind but the music and the movements. Finally, she knew she was ready. She held her arms out and released it.

"Vibro-shock!"

A slight visual distortion in the air was all Daniel had as a warning. "Everyone, watch out!" He called. "Get away from Geddon quickly." Everyone dove away as the incredible blast of vibration energy slowly but surely penetrated Geddon's shields and hit the front of Geddon. Geddon backed up to lessen the damage by Marta's attack but it still suffered damage.

"I did it," Marta gasped. Then, a smile slowly overtook her frown. I did it!"

Sage Mattonda watched it all from up above. His only thought: *King Gladirus is very smart.* Most magic attributes are divided into two categories: physical which means the magic can be channeled through the body and ethereal, meaning it could be released in some sort of elemental or energy attack. The red eyes on Geddon's towers enabled it to recognize the difference between physical and ethereal magic and retaliate accordingly. That was the secret behind Geddon's never-ending power. But Marta, her magic is special. It is neither physical nor ethereal, but a hybrid of the two. Such a quality was very rare; only one in twenty random people would have a hybrid magic. Geddon wasn't able to tell if it was physical or ethereal and therefore, couldn't mount an effective counter-offense or even a put up a successful defense strategy. Sage Mattonda had to admit, this was something he hadn't counted on, someone who wasn't a Sage penetrating Geddon's defenses, but it would not affect the final part of his plan. Soon, it would be time for him to make an appearance and after that; it will be smooth sailing for him.

Marta was still shocked at her ability to pierce the barrier surrounding Geddon and hit its armor.

"Marta, that was incredible," Daniel commented. "How did you do that? I thought no magic could penetrate it."

"Marta's magic is special. The Guardians must've taken special care when blessing her with a magic," King Gladirus commented. Even Andros had to admit that Marta's action was impressive. He began to feel something he had heard people talk about but never experienced until now: admiration. He admired the young girl who at first wanted to kill King Gladirus, and now doing her best in trying to save his kingdom.

"Everyone, look," Maran called. Geddon had recovered from being attacked and had continued on its way. It was now on the edge of the city. Ada transformed into a giant troll and stood in front of Geddon. Ada pushed hard on Geddon's outer armor, trying to push it back.

"Marta, use your powers one more time," King Gladirus instructed.

"But are you sure my powers will beat it this time?" Marta asked.

"With a little help, it will. Just start."

Marta had no reason to doubt King Gladirus, especially not now. She began her dance once again, this time putting her whole soul into each movement.

Andros was in awe at Marta's movements. He never really paid much attention to them until now. They were so strong, yet so beautiful, almost like Marta herself. Andros placed a hand on his stomach. His heart, it was as if he was feeling it beat for the very first time. King Gladirus was right about one thing, Marta is special. He then noticed that King Gladirus was also making strange movements and some of them were similar to Marta's. He immediately put two and two together. "Is it possible?"

It was.

"Marta, release all your energy now!" King Gladirus ordered. Marta complied and King Gladirus released the energy that he had gathered.

"Vibro-shock!" They both cried.

"I don't believe it!" Daniel gasped. "King Gladirus has the same magic as Marta!" It was true; King Gladirus had the vibro-shock powers, the same as Marta. The two vibro-shock magic intertwined with one another. Geddon, who had thrown Ada into a couple of houses with its claw, took it full force. The red jewels stopped glowing and cracked.

"It's finally over," Marta said collapsing to the ground. Using two vibro-shocks simultaneously was very draining on her. "It's finally... over."

"I don't think it's over yet," Andros said. He pointed to the jewel on Geddon's central tower which was beginning to flicker back to life.

Marta moaned. "No more, please, Guardians, no more."

"Get ready, everyone," Andros warned drawing both his daggers. Anánzu cocked an arrow, and threw a new sword to Captain Vostock who stood side-by-side with Captain Garan, ready for combat.

Suddenly Sage Mattonda landed in between them. Marta gasped. What was Sage Mattonda trying to do? Was he trying to redeem himself for awaking Geddon, destroying Gerard and attacking them? Or was this simply part of his nefarious plot? Either way, Marta was too tired to do anything about it.

Sage Mattonda aimed his staff at Geddon and fired a bolt of energy. Because Geddon was already weak from Marta's and King Gladirus' attacks, it was pushed back. Sage Mattonda twirled his staff a couple of times before slamming the jewel end on the ground. Energy traveled through the ground and erupted underneath Geddon causing it to topple over. Sage Mattonda drove the pointed end of his staff into the ground and called out, "Tel-ána envelpus!" A crack formed from the Sage to Geddon and a chasm opened up underneath the weapon and Geddon fell into the abyss. The chasm closed, crushing Geddon like an egg shell underneath an armored boot.

Sage Mattonda turned towards the battle-weary heroes. For a moment, it looked like he was going to attack them, especially when he started walking towards Marta. But to everyone's surprise, he walked right by them and went over to a man who was on the ground.

"Are you all right?" The Sage asked the man.

"Yes, thank you, Sage, I am grateful you are here."

"It will always be my mission to protect the people of Tel-ána, no matter what kingdom they are in," Sage Mattonda said.

King Gladirus let out a chuckle. "I finally understand," he said. "All this was a ploy to discredit me and establish himself as ruler of Tel-ána. Once the people learn that he defeated the undefeatable weapon, they will demand the crown from me."

"We can't let him do that," Daniel protested. "Let's tell the people what we found out, they will believe us."

"No," King Gladirus said. "If he wants the throne so much, then it shall be his."

Captain Garan argued, "You deserve to rule, you and Marta defeated the unstoppable Geddon!"

"I'm sorry, noble Captain, but it is past my time. I am too old to be ruling in these rapidly changing times. Perhaps he will make a better ruler than me."

"It's not just that," Captain Vostock threw in. "Once the other kingdoms discover what happened, they will want to form alliances with him, because becoming allies with a kingdom controlled by the Sage who defeated Geddon is more beneficial than making an enemy out of one. Sage Mattonda had just single-handedly taken over Tel-ána."

"Well, one good thing did come out of this," Andros said trying to lighten the mood. "I'm no longer in danger of being hanged."

"And my daughter's killer has been avenged," Anánzu threw in. "At last, I can sleep peacefully tonight."

"I didn't do it," Marta said attracting everyone's attention. Her voice was surprisingly calm. "I wasn't able to avenge the destruction of Gerard, and I wasn't able to stop Sage Mattonda from taking over. But you know... it's like what Andros said, something good did come out of all of this." She looked around. "I met all of you, and that was worth losing the chance of revenge. I may have lost my old family, but..." Marta wiped the tears from her eyes. They were happy tears. "In the process, I gained a new one."

"Marta," Daniel said stepping forward. "What will happen to us now?"

Marta smiled and embraced her cousin. Her voice sounded older than a twelve year old. "We go on, Daniel. We go on, like we always do."

"Look." Everybody looked to the sky. A single ray of light was piercing the clouds. It was like the Guardians were giving their blessing on their decision this day, their decision to allow Sage Mattonda to go through with his plan. It was like they were saying that it would be a decision that they would not regret.

And so it came to past, in the world of Tel-ána, that a secret war was fought, but never won. But the experience gained and friendships made this day will live on with the unlikely group of young heroes. And they will need it, for this was not the end. On the contrary, this was only the beginning.

The saga will continue in Magic: The Rising Darkness

Printed in the United States
by Baker & Taylor Publisher Services